CLAP HANDS, HERE COMES CHARLIE

'Prison wasn't the worst part,' he said.

She frowned up into his face.

'Not knowing was the worst part,' he tried to explain, with difficulty. 'Being aware, as I was, for almost a year that I was being hunted yet not knowing what they were doing or how to fight back . . .'

He paused, back among the memories.

'Not knowing is like being aware that you're dying and unable to do anything about it,' he said.

For several moments, neither spoke. Then Berenkov said: 'And Charlie's got to live like that forever.'

'Unless he's caught,' she reminded him.

'Unless he becomes careless and is caught,' he agreed.

Clap Hands,
Here Comes Charlie

BRIAN FREEMANTLE

ARROW BOOKS

Arrow Books Limited
62–65 Chandos Place, London WC2N 4NW

An imprint of Century Hutchinson Limited

London Melbourne Sydney Auckland
Johannesburg and agencies throughout
the world

First published in Great Britain by Jonathan Cape Ltd 1978
Sphere edition 1979
Arrow edition 1987

Printed and bound in Great Britain by
Anchor Brendon Limited, Tiptree, Essex

ISBN 0 09 951780 9

For Toby and Pauline,
with much love

'Oh well, this is a can of worms as you know a lot of this stuff that went on. And the people who worked this way are awfully embarrassed . . . but the way you have handled all this seems to me has been very skilful, putting your fingers in the leaks that have sprung here and sprung there.'

Former President Richard Nixon to John Dean, his then counsel, September 15, 1972, from the submission of recorded Presidential conversations to the Committee of Judiciary of the House of Representatives.

His hand will be against every man
and every man's hand against him

Genesis

ONE

The third turning would mean he would be going back the way he had come. He took it as a test and when they kept in step Charlie Muffin knew they were following.

The fear belched up, sour in the back of his throat, like the brandy sickness every morning.

'Oh, Christ,' he said, desperately.

So it was to be disguised as a backstreet brawl. Scuffling, grunting men, fighting expertly. Back against a slimy wall. No escape. Clawing for the knife-hand, stomach bunched and tight against the first searing burst of pain. No sound. Not words, anyway. Only in the end, perhaps. Before they fled. Traitor, they'd say. So he would know they'd got him. At last.

The road was narrow, hardly more than an alley, leading back towards the Sacré Cœur he could see outlined blackly on top of the Montmartre hill. High, anonymous buildings either side. No people. And dark..Jesus, it was dark.

He'd actually made it easy for them. Careless again. Like Edith kept saying.

Behind, the footsteps quickened, as they recognised the opportunity.

He tried to move faster, too, but it was difficult. The road had begun to steepen, with the final gradient before the steps up to the massive Paris landmark; hand-rails were set into the walls for support. He snatched out, hauling himself along. Shoulders heaving, he stopped, winded and panting, looking back. About fifty yards, he guessed. Surprised they were so far away. Moving steadily, though. Sure of themselves. No hurry now. After all these months, they'd found him.

The break in the wall actually alarmed him, so that he pulled away from it, whimpering. If it led into an enclosed courtyard, he would be trapped. Charlie could hear them

9

now, much closer. More noise than he would have expected.

He pushed into the opening, the relief moaning from him when he saw the narrow rectangle of light at the far end from a parallel road. It was one that the tourists climbed to the cathedral, lined with bars and souvenir shops. And with people.

At last the neglected training, so deeply instilled it was almost instinct, began to take over from the initial terror. So he didn't run.

Why the fifty-yard gap? And the unnecessary noise? And this, a passageway to safety?

It meant they weren't professionals. And that he'd panicked. So he wasn't professional. Not any more.

At the entry to the broader street he paused, letting himself be silhouetted, then went right, at the sound of their suddenly scurrying footsteps. He was already inside the bar when they thrust out, looking wildly in both directions. Itinerant North Africans, he identified immediately. Knitted headpieces, pulled down over their ears, second-hand westernised clothes, threadbare and greasy. Muggers, he guessed. Frightened, nervous illiterates trying to catch an unsuspecting tourist in a back alley and grab enough money for a cockroach-infested blanket or maybe a roll of kif.

And Charlie Muffin, who had fought and defeated the intelligence systems of England and America, had collapsed. No, he certainly wasn't professional any more.

Angrily he swilled the rest of the cognac into his mouth, gagging slightly as it caught at the back of his throat. He could still taste the sourness of his fear.

Outside, the two men shrugged, looked around uncertainly and finally moved into an opposite bar.

Charlie gestured and when the waiter came, asked for a *jeton* for the telephone. He waited until his glass was refilled and then moved to the corner booth, jiggling the coin between his fingers.

He'd already started on his third drink by the time the police responded to his anonymous call and swept into the café opposite. He'd reported the men as drug pedlars, guessing one of them would be carrying kif. If not, then it was a reasonable bet their papers wouldn't be in order. Either way, it didn't matter. By the time they were released, they would have been as frightened as he had been an hour earlier.

He snorted at his own reflection in the mirror behind the zinc-topped bar. Some victory. But it had been even more instinctive than the training. Anyone who attacked Charlie Muffin had to be attacked in response. And hurt more.

It was time to move on, he decided abruptly. Edith wouldn't mind leaving Paris. Welcome it, in fact. She had always preferred Zürich.

'Another cognac?' enquired the barman.

'Why not?' said Charlie.

Because he got drunk and made mistakes, he answered himself. It didn't seem to matter. Whatever he did, it wouldn't be as disastrous as the mistake he'd already made. And from which he could never recover.

It was a rotten existence, thought Charlie.

TWO

Alexei Berenkov preferred the dacha in the autumn evenings, about an hour before it got truly dark. Then he could look down from the Moscow hills and see the Soviet capital swaddled in its smoky, protective mist, like a Matisse painting. He wondered what had happened to the one he had had in the lounge of the Belgravia house. Sold, probably. The British government would have made money, he knew. It had been a bargain when he bought it. The furniture would have gone up in value, too. Certainly the French Empire.

He heard movement and turned expectantly, smiling at Valentina. His wife was a plump, comfortable woman, warm to be next to on a winter's night. Wouldn't have been quite the same near the Mediterranean. Or in Africa, perhaps. But then, he thought, he wasn't near the Mediterranean. Or Africa. Nor would he be, ever again.

'Happy?' she asked.

'Completely.'

'I never thought it would end like this. So perfectly, I mean.'

Berenkov didn't reply immediately.

'Were you very frightened?' he asked.

'Always,' she replied. 'I expected it to get better, when you'd established yourself with a good cover. But it didn't. It got worse. When I heard you'd been arrested, it was almost a relief . . . the news I'd expected for so long.'

He nodded.

'I was getting very nervous, too, towards the end,' he admitted.

'Was prison very bad?'

He nodded again.

'I knew I'd never serve the full sentence, of course,' he said. 'I thought, in the beginning, that I would be able to withstand it easily enough, waiting for the exchange that we always arrange . . . but it had a strange, destructive effect . . .'

Valentina looked at the man she had seen so rarely in the past twenty years. The furtive, cowed look had gone at last, she realised. Now the only legacy was the hair, completely white. Once it had been so black, she remembered nostalgically. My Georgian bear, she had called him. She reached out, feeling for his arm, looking down with him over the faraway city.

'What was Charlie Muffin like?' she asked unexpectedly.

He considered her question.

'A very unusual man,' he said firmly. 'Very unusual indeed.'

'I owe him so much,' said the woman. 'And I'll never be able to thank him.'

'Neither will I,' said Berenkov.

'It would be nice to show my gratitude.'

'Yes,' agreed the man.

'Did you like him?'

'Very much,' he said, distantly. Then he added: 'And now I feel sorry for him.'

'Sorry?'

'He was very clever, doing what he did. But I'm sure he never completely realised what it would be like afterwards.'

He shivered, a man suddenly exposed to the cold.

'. . . more terrible than prison,' he said. 'Far more terrible.'

It had been stupid to begin the conversation, she decided, irritated with herself. It had led to needless reminiscence and they had been getting away from that in the last few months.

'It's all over now,' she said briskly. 'And we can forget about it.'

'I'll never be able to do that,' he said. 'Nor want to.'

'Just prison, then,' she accepted. 'The worst part.'

He looked down at the woman, smiling at her misunderstanding.

'Prison wasn't the worst part,' he said.

She frowned up into his face.

'Not knowing was the worst part,' he tried to explain, with difficulty. 'Being aware, as I was, for almost a year that I was being hunted yet not knowing what they were doing or how to fight back . . .'

He paused, back among the memories.

'Not knowing is like being aware that you're dying and unable to do anything about it,' he said.

For several moments, neither spoke. Then Berenkov said: 'And Charlie's got to live like that forever.'

'Unless he's caught,' she reminded him.

'Unless he becomes careless and is caught,' he agreed.

THREE

It was an unfortunate coincidence, each event detracting from the other. On balance, there was far more ceremony and pomp about the inauguration of the American President so the coverage from Washington unquestionably overshadowed the election victory of the British Premier.

Comparison was inevitable, of course. Radio and television commentators maintained a constant interchange of fact and fallacy to make their points and from the grave that provided complete surveillance of the cemetery the man sighed irritably, knowing there would be no other subject covered that day.

He had never before switched the softly tuned transistor lodged against the headstone to anything but continuous news coverage or talk programmes. He looked around and saw some genuine mourners only yards away; they'd be bound to hear any pop music. Damn it.

Still, remembered the man, it had been worse in the early days. He hadn't thought of bringing the radio then, even for boring current affairs debates. Or evolved the method he now employed to pass the time. Other shifts had copied him and there wasn't a better-kept burial spot in the graveyard. He felt quite proud. No one had said anything officially, though. Hadn't really expected them to; civil servants were a miserable lot.

His jacket lay neatly folded and far enough away to avoid it being splashed by water from his bucket or scrubbing brushes. He knelt on a specially padded piece of blanket and cleaned to a slow rhythm, a regular metronome movement, forward and back, forward and back.

' . . . bright new future from the gloom of the past . . .' intoned the American President, Henry Austin, and the undertaking was relayed instantly by satellite from the podium on Pennsylvania Avenue to the churchyard in Sussex.

What sort of future did he have? wondered the grave-cleaner. Damn all, he decided. His gloom of the past would be the gloom of the future.

Some clumsy so-and-so had chipped the bordering granite near the headstone, he saw.

'Sorry, love,' he said.

He frequently wondered about Harriet Jamieson, spinster, who had died on the 13th of October, 1932, aged 61 years and been buried in the hope of eternal peace. Probably a relation of someone in the department, he had decided. Otherwise there might have been a query about all the care being expended on the grave.

'Bet you didn't have so many men sweating over you when you were alive, Harriet my girl,' he said.

The radio programme switched to the B.B.C.'s Westminster studio. The new Premier had made a brief Commons appearance, said the reporter, his voice urgent to make the event sound more exciting than it had really been.

' . . . time to bind our wounds . . .' said the commentator, quoting Arthur Smallwood's message verbatim.

'Good grief,' quietly muttered the man in the cemetery.

He heard the church clock strike and rose gratefully. There was a telephone just outside the lychgate and he was connected immediately.

'Nothing, as always,' he reported.

'Thank you,' replied the duty clerk.

'Someone's chipped the surround, near the headstone.'

'I'll make a note of it.'

'I don't want to be held responsible.'

'I said I'd record it.'

'How much longer are we going to keep this up, for Christ's sake?'

'Until we're instructed otherwise,' said the clerk.

Prissy bastard, thought the man, as he went off duty.

In Washington, Henry Austin gazed over the crowds that

lined the avenue right up to the White House, happy in the politician's knowledge that the inaugural address had caught just the right note.

'I come to office,' said the new President, 'intending to honour the pledge I have made several times during this campaign to the American people. The mistakes of the past will be corrected ... when necessary with the utmost vigour. And I will do my best to ensure that fewer are committed in the future ...'

And from the specially equipped room at Downing Street, Arthur Smallwood stared into the television cameras and out at the watching British people, his face grave with sincerity.

'... overcome accepted and difficult problems,' he said, coming to the conclusion of his address to the nation. 'They are inherited from the past. My government and I are confident that we can do better than that which we succeed. We are determined in that resolve. And prepared to be judged by you, the people, on our efforts ...'

'My God!' protested the grave-cleaner in familiar exasperation, leaning forward to snap off the television set on which he'd watched both events. 'That's all I've heard, all day. Empty politicians making empty bloody promises. And they haven't a clue what's going on. Not a clue.'

'Chops,' announced his wife, through the kitchen hatch of their semi-detached house in Dulwich. 'I've got pork chops. Is that all right?''

The man didn't answer. He'd get the blame for that damaged grave, he knew. Charlie Muffin was a bloody nuisance.

Henry Austin enjoyed it all, the speech and the triumphal drive to the mansion that was to be his home for the next four years and the photographic session and the reception and the grand ball.

'Brilliant speech, Mr President,' Willard Keys, the Secretary of State, congratulated him.

'I meant what I said,' replied Austin seriously. They were in the corner of the ballroom, momentarily away from most of the guests.

'Mr President?'

'About mistakes. I want this administration squeaky clean. And I want everyone to understand that. Everyone.'

'I'll see to it.'

'And Willard.'

'Mr President?'

'I mean the past as well. I don't want any embarrassments that we're not prepared for. Make that clear, too. Everything tidied up . . . no loose ends.'

'Why don't we make it the first policy memorandum from the Oval Office?'

'Yes,' agreed the President. 'Why don't we?'

Four thousand miles away, Arthur Smallwood stared across the first-floor study at Downing Street, inviting the Foreign Secretary's assessment.

'Good,' judged William Heyden. Feeling he should say more he added: 'Pity about the American inauguration.'

'Couldn't be helped,' said Smallwood, philosophically.

The two men sipped their whisky.

'It isn't going to be easy,' admitted Smallwood, suddenly. 'I made a number of promises because I had to. There will be a lot of people waiting for the first slip.'

'Yes,' agreed Heyden, who thought the Premier had over-committed them but didn't know the man well enough to suggest criticism. 'We'll have to watch ourselves.'

'We must let the departments and ministries know the new feeling,' said Smallwood. 'Particularly the permanent people who think they can ignore us and make their own policy.'

'A gentle hint?' said Heyden carelessly.

'No,' Smallwood corrected him immediately. 'A positive directive.'

FOUR

The mid-Channel passport check was always the most dangerous part, the moment when, despite the previous occasions, there could be a sudden challenge and they would be trapped aboard the ship, unable to run.

They had learned to time the public announcement about the immigration office and in the last few minutes preceding it Edith became increasingly nervous, sitting tense and upright and abandoning any attempt at conversation. There were no outward signs from Charlie, except perhaps in the way he drank the habitual brandy, not in spaced-out, even sips, but in deep swallows, so that the barman had already recognised him as a drinker and was standing close at hand, waiting for the nod.

They made an odd couple, she restrained, carefully coiffured and with the discreet but expensively maintained elegance of a Continental woman unafraid of obvious middle age, he baggy and shapeless in a nondescript suit, like a dustcover thrown over a piece of anonymous furniture about which nobody cared very much.

Edith started up at the metallic-voice broadcast, coming immediately to Charlie for guidance. Unspeaking, he led the way out into the purser's square, then paused by the perfume and souvenir shop.

'Don't worry,' he encouraged her.

She appeared not to hear.

What he wanted appeared almost immediately and he smiled at Edith. She looked back, without expression.

The smaller child was already crying, overtired and demanding to be carried. The mother, face throbbing red and split by sunburn, tried to push it away and by mistake hit the other girl, who started crying too, and immediately an argument began between the woman and her husband.

'Perfect,' judged Charlie.

He moved quickly now, his hand cupping Edith's elbow. He could feel the nervousness tighten within her as they wedged themselves behind the squabbling family and began edging closer to the immigration office.

'It'll be all right,' he assured her emptily. She remained stiff by his side, staring straight ahead.

The children caused the expected distraction, filling the tiny room with noise. The parents' row spilled over to the immigration officer at a query about the children being entered on both passports and Charlie and Edith passed through in the wake of the official's anticipated anxiety to regain order in the file of people.

'Works every time,' said Charlie, still holding Edith's arm and leading her back towards the bar. She was still very frightened, he knew.

In recent months she had shown her concern at his drinking by almost total abstinence, but she accepted the brandy now, gulping at it.

'It's been too long,' he said. 'They will have abandoned the blanket scrutiny long ago. And there's nothing wrong with the passports.'

She shook her head, refusing the lie.

'That's nonsense and you know it. They'll never give up. Not until you're dead.'

'This is the fifth time we've crossed from the Continent without any trouble.'

She shrugged, still not accepting the reassurance.

'Thank God we won't have to go through it again.'

'We're safe, I tell you.'

With his empty glass, he gestured to the attentive barman, waving away the change.

'If you're so safe, why are you drunk every night by ten o'clock?' she demanded. It was an unfair question, Edith realised. Fear wasn't the only reason. But she wanted to hurt him, desperate for any reaction that would cause him to stop. She was very worried at the growing carelessness. She should be grateful, she supposed, that he'd finally agreed to abandon England. It had taken enough arguments.

He smiled, a lopsided expression.

'Nothing else to do,' he said, answering her question.

Edith shook her head, sadly.

'You know something, Charlie?' she said.

He drank awkwardly, spilling some of the liquor down his suit. It was already stained, she saw.

'What?'

'I never thought I would feel sorry for you. Amost every other emotion, probably. But never pity. And that's nearly all there is now, Charlie. Pity.'

Another attempt to hurt, she recognised. Because it wasn't true.

'What about love?'

'You're making it difficult,' she persisted. 'Very difficult.'

He tried to straighten, to conceal the extent of his drunkenness, then discarded the pretence, slumping round-shouldered in the chair.

'Thank you for agreeing to leave England,' she said sincerely. The gesture was for her, she accepted.

Charlie shrugged, knowing the words would jam if he tried to speak. She had been right in persuading him, he knew. They were both much happier in Zürich, and having dispensed with Paris there wasn't much point in retaining the Brighton house either. That was the trouble, he decided, extending the thought; there didn't seem much point in anything any more.

'We've still got to get nearly £300,000 out of England,' he said. 'Won't you be frightened?'

'Yes,' she said. It would be wrong to suggest he just left it and lived on the money she had, she knew.

'Won't you be?' she asked.

He humped his shoulders, an uncaring gesture.

'Perhaps,' he said. He nodded and the refilled glass dutifully appeared.

He probably wouldn't recall the conversation in the morning, decided Edith. It was already long past remembering time . . . long past many things.

Charlie was bored, she recognised. Bored and uninterested. For someone who had led a life as unique as Charlie's, it was like an illness, gradually weakening him. Now he had nothing. Except guilt. There was a lot of that, she knew.

'Promise me something else,' she tried, hopefully, as the ferry began to move alongside the Southampton quayside.

His eyes were filmed, she saw, and his face was quite unresponsive.

'Don't go to the grave,' she pleaded. 'It's a stupid, sentimental pilgrimage. He wouldn't have expected you to do it.'

'Want to,' said Charlie, stubbornly.

'It's ridiculous, Charlie. There's absolutely no point. And you know it.'

'We're coming here for the last time,' he reminded her. 'So I'm going, just once. I've waited long enough. It'll be safe now.'

She sighed, accepting defeat.

'Oh Charlie,' she said. 'Why does it all have to be such an awful mess?'

The office of George Wilberforce, Director of British Intelligence, was on the corner of the Whitehall building that gave views over both the Cenotaph and Parliament Square.

It was a darkly warm, reassuring room, in which the oil paintings of bewigged and satined statesmen adorning the panelled walls seemed an unnecessary reminder of an Empire.

The modern innovation of double glazing excluded noise from outside and deep pile carpet succeeded within. The books were in hand-tooled leather and the massive desk at which Wilberforce sat had been salvaged in 1947 aboard the same vessel that brought home the Queen's throne from an independent India. Wilberforce considered he had the more comfortable piece of furniture.

The Director appeared as tailored for the room as the antique furniture and the unread first editions. He was a fine-featured, elegantly gangling man who affected pastel coloured shirts with matching socks and a languid diffidence that concealed the fervent need for acceptance in a job he had coveted for fifteen years and seen to go to two other men before him.

The only intrusive mannerism was the habit, during acrimonious or difficult discussions, of using a briar pipe, which he was never seen to light, like worry-beads, revolving it between his peculiarly long fingers and constantly exploring the bowl with a set of tiny tools that retreated into a gold container.

'It's good to see you again,' greeted Wilberforce formally. Always before the meetings had been in Washington: he couldn't recall an American Director of the C.I.A. making a visit like this to his predecessors, he thought.

Onslow Smith responded with one of the open-faced, boyish smiles that Wilberforce recalled from the sports photographs that littered the man's office.

'Seemed a good idea to hitch a ride on the same aircraft taking the new vice-President on his tour of Europe,' said the C.I.A. director.

Wilberforce looked doubtful and the other man's smile became apologetic.

'And there was another reason,' he conceded.

'What?'

Smith hesitated, arranging the words.

'The President has a new broom complex,' he said. 'Just like your guy.'

He cleared his throat, to make the quote obvious.

' ... "loose ends neatly tied ... mistakes vigorously rectified where necessary."'

Already, recalled Wilberforce, political cartoonists were featuring Austin and Smallwood taking turns at being each other's ventriloquist's dummies.

'So I hear,' said the Briton, waiting.

'There's been an official policy document,' said Smith.

'We've had something like that here,' admitted Wilberforce.

'Which means we have the same old problem,' said Onslow Smith.

Wilberforce nodded, reaching out for a worry pipe.

'Charlie Muffin,' he agreed. 'The bastard.'

FIVE

It wasn't until he got into the churchyard and felt the damp, cold wind that always seems to blow in English cemeteries in November that Charlie Muffin sobered sufficiently to realise completely what he had done. And that the stupidity could kill him. Like so many stupidities before it.

The trained instinct surfaced through the swamp of alcohol and he pulled away from one of the main pathways, using a straggled yew tree for cover. About ten yards away, a black knot of people huddled speechless around a grave still cheerfully bright from funeral flowers. Nearer, a practised mourner, shirt-sleeved despite the cold, knelt over a green-pebbled rectangle on a padded cloth, scrubbing the headstone and surround into its original whiteness, lips moving in familiar conversation with someone who couldn't reply any more. Charlie turned, widening his vision. At least twenty people spread throughout the churchyard. Too many.

'You're a prick,' Charlie told himself. 'A right prick.'

He frowned, surprised at the emergence of the habit. He'd always talked to himself, unashamedly, when he was under stress or afraid. It had been a long time since he had done it. Like welcoming back an old friend, he thought.

The drunkenness was gone now, but the pain was banded around his head and his throat was dehydrated. For a man apparently seeking a momentarily forgotten grave, he'd stood long enough beneath the tree, Charlie decided, groping for the professionalism of which he had once been so confident. He swallowed, forcing back the desire to flee, to run back along the wider pathway to the car he could still see, over the low wall.

'Never run,' he murmured. 'Never ever run.'

One of the basic lessons. Often ignored, though. Sometimes by people who should know better. And invariably by amateurs. Günther Bayer had been an amateur. No, Charlie corrected, not an amateur. An innocent. A trusting, manipulated innocent who had believed Charlie was sincere in trying to help him escape across the Wall. And so he'd run when he got caught in the East German ambush that had been intended for Charlie. He'd been dead before the flames had engulfed the Volkswagen, Charlie assured himself. Had to be, in that cross-fire.

He pushed away from the tree, rejoining the main path, alert for the attention the movement would have caused even a trained watcher. Nothing. Perhaps he was all right, after all. Perhaps, after so long, there was no observation. Or perhaps they were too well trained.

The pathway along which he was walking ran parallel with the perimeter wall, Charlie realised. But there was a linking lane, built like a spoke through the middle. He could turn on to that and regain the entrance. Four hundred yards, he estimated. It seemed a very long way.

The hesitation was hardly perceptible when, suddenly, he saw the tomb. In his earlier drunkenness he had imagined that Sir Archibald Willoughby's grave would be marked in an ordinary, traditional way, like that tended by the shirt-sleeved man near the yew tree. The family vault was an ornate, castellated affair, protected by an iron fence and reached through a low, locked gate. Plaques were set into the wall, recording the names of the occupants.

Charlie was confident his reaction to the vault had been completely covered; to stop, pause, even, would be all the confirmation they would need.

He was past, actually on the straight path leading to the exit, when the challenge came.

'Charlie! Charlie Muffin!'

Afterwards Charlie remembered with satisfaction the

smoothness of his reactions. The gateway was still too far away to consider walking on, as if the name meant nothing. He couldn't run, of course. But they could. They'd get him before he'd gone twenty yards. They? It had been a single voice. Just one man, after so long? Probably. Fight then. Feign bewilderment, to gain the moment of uncertainty. Then fight to kill. Quickly, before anyone in the cemetery realised what was happening. Go for the throat, the carotid artery, smashing the voice box with the same blow. Sir Archibald's tomb would give him the concealment. He'd only need minutes to get to the car.

He tensed, to make the turn, then stopped. There'd been all the training, certainly. Poncing about in canvas suits, waving his arms about and yelling 'aargh' like a bloody idiot. But he'd never killed anyone – not body to body, feeling the warmth of their skin and possibly seeing the terror in their faces. That had always been done by proxy, by others.

He completed the turn, head held curiously, keeping the movement purposely slow.

'I'm sorry ...' he frowned, the confusion perfectly balanced.

It was a tall man, habitually stooped in an effort to reduce his size. Beaked nose, too large for his face. A clipped, military moustache, a darker brown than the swept-back, short-cropped hair. Familiar, decided Charlie. Someone from the old department then. The man smiled and began coming forward.

"It *is* Charlie Muffin, isn't it?"

He wasn't professional, judged Charlie. Couldn't be. What properly trained man openly challenged a victim? And then walked forward, both arms held out, losing any chance of surprise in producing a weapon? He wouldn't make another juvenile mistake like Paris, Charlie decided.

Who then?

'Willoughby,' the man identified himself, as if in answer to Charlie's question. 'Rupert Willoughby.'

Charlie's eyes flickered for a moment to the name on the

tomb plaques, then back to the man who was now offering his hand, recognising the similarity. The handshake was firm, without the usual ridiculous tendency to turn it into a form of Indian palm wrestling, and the brown eyes held Charlie's in a direct, almost unblinking gaze. Just like the old man's, remembered Charlie. Until the end, that was.

'What an incredible coincidence,' said Willoughby.

'Yes,' agreed Charlie, the confusion genuine now.

Immediately fear swept it aside. If the graveyard were still under surveillance, then now he had been positively identified, he realised. Sir Archibald's son would be known, to all of them. And they were standing immediately outside the vault, the marker he'd managed to avoid only minutes earlier. He still had a little time, he decided. Not much. But still enough to use.

He tried to withdraw his hand, turning back to the gate.

' ... decided to pay my respects,' he stumbled, badly. 'Haven't been able to, before ... in a hurry, though. Really must go.'

'No, please, wait,' protested Willoughby. 'There's a great deal for us to discuss ... a business matter ...'

'Perhaps another time ... sorry, I'm very late ...'

Willoughby was walking with him, frowning at the rudeness. He reached into his pocket and Charlie edged away, apprehensively. The man produced a small wallet and offered Charlie a card.

'We must meet again,' he said. 'It's most important ... to do with my father ...'

'Call you,' promised Charlie, thrusting the pasteboard into his pocket. He was almost at the exit now. The obvious place, he decided; the lychgate would certainly provide some cover and they could get him away in a car before anyone in the cemetery realised the attack had happened. Charlie paused, examining it. There was no one there.

'Promise?' demanded Willoughby.

Charlie turned to the man, realising the need to recover.

'I really am very sorry,' he said, stopping with his back to the support pole for the gate roof, positioning himself where he could see the beginning of any approach. 'It must seem very rude.'

Willoughby didn't reply, confirming the assessment.

'Like to spend more time . . . believe me.'

'Call me then?'

'Of course.'

'When?'

'Soon,' promised Charlie hurriedly, turning through the gate. The mourners he had seen around the fresh grave were dispersing, heads bowed, into various cars. A woman was crying. The man who had been scrubbing the surround had finished, too, he saw. Carefully the man had packed the brush, cloths and bucket into the boot of an old Morris and was walking slowly towards the telephone.

'I'll be waiting,' called Willoughby, after him.

Charlie drove alert for the slightest danger, eyes constantly scanning the rear view mirror. Purposely he went north-west, choosing Tunbridge Wells because it was the first town of any size, twisting and turning through the streets and then continuing north, to London, to repeat the evasion.

'You're a prick, Charlie,' he accused himself again, as he took the car over Vauxhall Bridge. 'A careless, idiot prick who deserves to die.'

He'd arranged to clear out the bank the following morning. But that didn't matter now. Only survival mattered.

'Prick,' he said.

The London home and elegant, sophisticated refuge of George Wilberforce was a second-floor apartment overlooking Eaton Square. Here, from Monday to Friday, he lived, returning only at the weekends to a nagging, condescending wife who refused him the respect that everyone seemed to find so difficult, and from whom he would have welcomed divorce but for the admittedly remote but nevertheless possible harm such an event might have caused his career. Those responsible for appointments in the permanent civil service were known sometimes to possess strong religious views and it was wise not to take chances.

Particularly not now. Because now his career was more assured than it had ever been.

Delius, he decided, would suit his mood.

Apart from the habit with never-smoked pipes, the Director was a man who rarely betrayed any emotion, but now after standing for several movements by the stereo unit he suddenly moved away in a halting, stiff-jointed attempt at what appeared to be a waltz. He stopped, embarrassed by his efforts.

'I've got you, Charlie Muffin,' he said. 'And now you're going to suffer for what you did. Christ, you're going to suffer.'

SIX

George Wilberforce blinked at the gritty sensation behind his eyes, knowing he should have allowed more time after the flight from London before this conference in the C.I.A. complex in the Virginia countryside. But this time he had wanted the meeting in America; to arrive the courier of news for which they had waited so long and sense the approbation, even if there were no open praise.

"You're quite sure?" demanded Onslow Smith urgently. The American Director, whom he had had to tell in advance of the meeting, was a large open-faced man who seemed constantly restricted within the confines of an office chair, business suit and subdued tie. As if in apologetic explanation for his build, the wall behind his desk was patterned with sports pennants, shields and group pictures of the Yale rowing and boxing teams. The Onslow Smith smile was featured in all.

'Quite sure,' said Wilberforce, keeping the exhilaration from his voice. 'We've caught Charlie Muffin.'

'Thank God for that,' said Smith distantly. 'It's about goddamn time.'

Appearing suddenly aware that the remark could be construed as criticism, he added quickly: 'Congratulations.'

Wilberforce's shrug of uncaring dismissal was perfect.

'And now can we kill him?' demanded Garson Ruttgers.

Wilberforce came up from the pipe at which he had already begun probing, staring at the diminutive, frail-seeming American whose ambition to become, as chief of the C.I.A., what Edgar Hoover had been to the F.B.I., had been destroyed by Charlie Muffin. Ruttgers was an unsettling feature of the group, thought Wilberforce, watching the man light a cigarette from the stump of that which had preceded it, never once breaking the staring-eyed gaze across the table through clerk-like, half-lens spectacles. About Ruttgers there was an aura of unpredictability, thought the Briton. And something else. The man physically frightened him, Wilberforce realised, surprised.

'It's not quite as easy as that,' he said guardedly.

'Why not?' demanded Ruttgers.

The constant inhalation of nicotine had turned the man's false teeth yellow. Why, wondered Wilberforce, didn't the American soak the dentures in stain remover? His breath must smell appallingly.

'Yes, why?'

The repeated question in the unpleasantly recognisable, phlegmy tone, came from Wilberforce's right and he turned to Sir Henry Cuthbertson. The baronet was a bulky, cumbersome man proud of family links that went back to the service of James I, who had conferred the original baronetcy. He'd earned the D.S.O. in the Second World War and been seconded from the Chief of Staff council to revitalise Britain's intelligence system after the fading, twenty-five-year directorship of Sir Archibald Willoughby. And lost the job in less than a year. Four hundred years of honour wrecked in a few short months by a scruffy ex-grammar school boy with an irritating Mancunian accent and the distressing tendency not to change his shirt every day, reflected Wilberforce.

It was hardly surprising Cuthbertson and Ruttgers wanted Charlie Muffin's immediate assassination, thought Wilberforce. But neither had operated under the new governments. Or knew – because nobody knew – of Wilberforce's determination to make Charlie Muffin's capture a personal triumph.

'Because there mustn't be any mistake,' said the British Director simply.

'No,' agreed Onslow Smith hurriedly. 'No mistakes.'

To be convinced, the feelings of the two older men would have to be bruised, realised Wilberforce.

'Let's not forget,' he said, 'that the errors made with Charlie Muffin in the past were absolutely horrifying.'

Ruttgers and Sir Henry shifted, both discomforted at the prospect of being reminded.

'Four years ago,' said Wilberforce, 'the British uncovered in Europe the most successful Russian infiltration of NATO since the Second World War. The man who led their operation, Alexei Berenkov, was jailed for forty years. It was one of the worst disasters ever suffered by the Russians – so grave, in fact, that it came as little surprise to either America or Britain to learn, as they did within a year, that Valery Kalenin, operational chief of the K.G.B., wanted to flee for asylum to the West . . .'

'We're all aware of the history,' said Ruttgers, in an attempt to halt the other man.

'And now we must put it in proper perspective,' insisted Wilberforce. 'It was a deceit. A deceit conceived and operated by Charlie Muffin, working not for the British intelligence organisation that employed him, but with Kalenin. A deceit to expose not just ordinary agents, but the British and American Directors; for them to be seized and offered in exchange for the repatriation of Alexei Berenkov.'

The embarrassment, recalled Wilberforce, had been incredible after that numbing evening in the C.I.A. 'safe' house in Vienna when Kalenin had arrived not nervous and alone, as they had expected, but followed by a Russian commando team who had carried Ruttgers and Cuthbertson back across the Czechoslovakian border. Charlie Muffin had shown a surprising knowledge of psychology, judging the ambition of both men would drive them to such close involvement. Upon reflection, it seemed lunacy. He hadn't thought so at the time, though. That was something else no one was ever going to learn.

'The man is a traitor,' insisted Ruttgers. 'So he should be shot.'

'A traitor,' agreed Wilberforce. Legally so, he qualified. But aware as he was – and as Charlie Muffin had certainly been – that Cuthbertson had decided he could be abandoned at the East German border in the final stages of the Berenkov seizure, Wilberforce found the accusation difficult. Another reservation, never admitted to anyone. Any more than it had ever been admitted that it had been Charlie who had co-ordinated Berenkov's capture, fitting together the disparate jigsaw so cleverly that not only Berenkov but nearly everyone in the European cell was caught. Charlie, who had deserved first praise and then acceptance within the reorganised department Sir Henry was establishing. And who instead had realised that he had been selected for sacrifice in the final stages. Sir Henry would never concede he had decided Charlie should die, of course. Convenient amnesia wasn't a new affliction in the department

'But a traitor who should not be allowed to cause further embarrassments to either government,' Wilberforce added.

The irritation of Ruttgers and Cuthbertson was increasing, Wilberforce saw. The American fussily lighted yet another cigarette and the British baron twisted the family-crested ring on the little finger of his left hand as if seeking solace in a talisman of his family's greatness.

'That's vitally important,' said Onslow Smith, once more in immediate agreement.

'And we couldn't guarantee that by a simple elimination,'

declared Wilberforce. The American Director was definitely deferring to him, he decided.

'Why not?' demanded an unconvinced Ruttgers.

'To start with,' said Wilberforce, 'because he isn't in England. He was, very briefly. That's where we picked him up and from where we followed him back to Zürich."

'I don't see the problem,' argued Cuthbertson. 'What's wrong with killing the man in Switzerland?'

The British Director sighed. They were very obtuse, he thought. But then, they hadn't considered the long-term advantages as he had.

'Initially,' he said, 'the problem is risking an assassination in a country other than our own, where we could not ensure complete co-operation of the civil authorities.'

'We've done it dozens of times before,' disputed Ruttgers.

'Maybe so,' agreed Wilberforce. 'But not so soon after your President and my Prime Minister have pledged, publicly, that theirs are going to be open governments, free from unnecessary criticism.'

He paused. They still weren't accepting the reasoning, he knew.

'But more importantly,' he started again, 'we can't kill Charlie Muffin without knowing whether he has established any automatic release of information from, say, a bank vault that would compound the difficulties he has already caused. Don't forget how devious the damned man is.'

'There's no way we could do that, for Christ's sake,' objected Ruttgers.

'Oh, yes there is,' said Wilberforce, smiling. 'And it's the way to ensure that Charlie Muffin comes back to England like an obedient dog answering a whistle.'

He was going to enjoy himself, decided Wilberforce. Enjoy himself very much indeed.

Johnny Packer, who was never to learn the real reason for his good fortune or how closely his life was so very briefly to become linked with a man called Charlie Muffin, decided that the party to celebrate his release from Parkhurst was exactly right. Far better than he could have expected, in fact. He'd ruled there wouldn't be any rubbish, no amateur tearaways in their flash suits and cannonballs of money where the other sort should have been, to impress whatever slag they were trying to pull that night. But he hadn't been able to guarantee who *would* come. And that was the value of the party, showing how well he was regarded. Everyone was there, he saw. Everyone who mattered, anyway. Harry Rich, the soft-voiced Irishman, who'd personally put two people into the supports of the M-4 flyover while the concrete was still wet and was now the undisputed controller of the East End as far west as Farringdon Street; Herbie Pie, who had wept – though from pleasure, not remorse – carving the faces and the Achilles tendons during the last confrontation in Soho and now giggled at the rehearsed joke and said he had the whole place stitched up; even Andie Smythe, who rarely came this far east, silk-suited, smooth-haired and shiny-faced, looking always as if he'd been polished all over with a soft cloth before setting out for the nightly tours of the Mayfair casinos to receive what was rightfully his for ensuring that the unloading of the innocent was never violently interrupted.

Like an actor in a long-running play aware of his spot on stage at any one moment, Johnny stood stiffly in his two-day-old suit, away from the bar that had been erected in the upstairs room of The Thistle, nodding and smiling to everyone but getting involved in no prolonged conversation.

The positioning was decreed by the rules of such gatherings, as formalised as the steps of a medieval dance or the mating rituals of some species of African birds.

It was Herbie who broke away from the group, the appointed spokesman.

'Good to see you out, Johnny.'

'Thank you, Mr. Pie. Nice of everyone to come.'

'Always happy to come to such functions. Specially when it's kept to the right people.'

Johnny sighed at the reminder of why he had served five years in Parkhurst.

'No more amateurs who can't stop boasting about what they've done,' he promised.

'Hope not, Johnny,' said Pie. 'Craftsmen like you shouldn't take risks.'

And he wouldn't, any more, thought Johnny. If he were caught again through not taking sufficient care about the people he was working with, he'd go down for ten. Maybe longer.

'Any plans, Johnny?' enquired the other man.

'I'm in nó hurry, Mr Pie. Got to get myself together first.'

The man nodded.

'Still got the little house in Wimbledon?'

'Yes,' said Johnny. 'Neighbours think I've been working on a five-year contract in Saudi Arabia.'

Pie nodded again, the encounter concluded. Everything was to a formula, even the apparent small talk.

'So should anyone want you, they could contact you there?'

'Any time,' Johnny assured him, keeping the hope from his voice. 'Any time.'

'And no amateurs this time?'

'No amateurs,' promised Johnny.

A clear enough warning, Johnny decided. The repeated criticism meant they still doubted him. So no one would be visiting Wimbledon until he'd proved himself again, no matter if he were one of the three top safecrackers in London. He'd have to do something pretty remarkable to recover, he decided.

'I think you'll like it,' said Onslow Smith.

Wilberforce sipped the wine, nodding appreciatively. The other man was unquestionably accepting his leadership, he decided, gratified.

'Not French,' he judged.

'Californian,' agreed the American Director.

'Excellent,' said Wilberforce. Surrounding himself with sports mementoes was all part of a carefully maintained affectation on Smith's part, decided the other Director generously, an invitation for people to imagine his thinking and intelligence as muscled as his body. Which would have been a mistake. Smith's decision to involve Ruttgers in the meeting that morning, just as he had included Cuthbertson, showed they were both aware of the dangers of the operation upon which they were embarking. And were taking out insurance. Both he and Smith could afford to be magnanimous in the vengeance hunt; if it were successful, then both would gain sufficient credit because of their association, while the two men worst affected would salvage something of their reputations. But if anything went wrong, then the fault could be hopefully offloaded on to those already disgraced. Perhaps that was why Smith was letting him take the lead, he thought fleetingly.

'It *is* a bank, isn't it?' guessed the American, suddenly.

Wilberforce smiled. Definitely very intelligent.

'What made you realise that?'

'When Charlie Muffin walked out of the house in Vienna, leaving Ruttgers and Cuthbertson to be grabbed, he took with him $500,000 we'd provided in the belief it was what Kalenin wanted to cross over. But you didn't mention the money this morning. So you must know where he's hiding it ... along with anything else that might embarrass us.'

'Yes,' admitted Wilberforce. 'It's a bank. And I know which one.'

'How?'

'We picked him up in a cemetery. Eventually he went to a house in Brighton, where he collected a woman we've since identified as his wife. It was obviously a house they'd had for some time. From the voters' register we got the name they had assumed. From then on, it was merely a routine job of having a team of men posing as credit inspectors calling up all the banks in the area until we found an account. We didn't expect a safe deposit, though ... that's what has made me worry he might have tried to protect himself with some documents.'

Wilberforce paused. Just like the drunken sot of a previous Director, Sir Archibald Willoughby, had tried to do.

He hadn't succeeded, though: they'd sealed up that difficulty just as they'd erase this if it existed.

The American added more wine to both their glasses.

'You know something that surprises me?'

'What?' asked Wilberforce.

'That Charlie Muffin didn't go to Russia. He'd have been welcome enough there, for God's sake.'

Wilberforce sighed. It was increasingly obvious, he thought, why it would have to be he who initiated everything in this operation.

'But Russia is the last place he would have gone,' he tried to explain. 'Charlie Muffin wouldn't have regarded what he did as helping Russia. Any more than he would think of it, initially anyway, of being traitorous to Britain or America.'

Onslow Smith frowned curiously at the other man.

'What the hell was it then?'

'Charlie Muffin fighting back,' said Wilberforce. 'When he realised we were prepared to let him die.'

'This isn't going to be easy, is it?' said Smith thoughtfully.

'No,' said Wilberforce. 'But it's the only way we can guarantee there won't be problems.'

'And it's necessary for us to be personally involved, potentially dangerous as it is?'

He seemed to be seeking reassurances, thought Wilberforce.

'There's no one else we could trust with it.'

Onslow Smith nodded, slowly.

'You're right, of course,' he accepted.

He smiled uncertainly.

'I bet the President never had this in mind when he promised to correct mistakes with the utmost vigour,' mused the American.

'But that's exactly what we're doing,' encouraged Wilberforce. 'But neither he nor the Prime Minister will ever appreciate it.'

'If they did know,' said Smith, 'they'd be damned scared. Tell me, George, are you frightened?'

'Properly apprehensive,' answered Wilberforce evasively.

Somehow, he had decided, the British Premier *would* learn what had been done for him. When it was all safely concluded, of course.

The C.I.A. Director smiled across the table.

'I'm scared,' he admitted. 'I'm damned scared.'

SEVEN

He wasn't asleep, Edith knew. Any more than he had been the previous night at this time, just before dawn. Or the night before that. Any night, in fact, since the cemetery incident.

She breathed deeply, hoping Charlie wouldn't realise she was awake and start talking. If they talked, they'd row. It was too late for rows. And anyway, Charlie's response would be to fight back. Survival, he called it. She sighed, maintaining the pretence of sleep. The need to survive: Charlie's panacea for anything unpalatable.

She became annoyed with herself, recognising the criticism. She had no right to think like that, she thought. No right at all. They *had* decided that Charlie was a disposable embarrassment, someone who could be dumped because he didn't have the right accent or public school tie and was a remnant from another, discredited era. So he had had every justification for what he had done. Justification on the filthy terms within which they operated, anyway.

If only Charlie hadn't stopped believing that. Poor Charlie. No matter what explanation or reasoning he advanced, he could never lose the feeling of remorse that had grown during the last year. Misplaced remorse, she thought. Because Charlie Muffin wasn't a traitor. An opportunist, she accepted. Amoral, too. Worryingly so. But no traitor. He couldn't dislodge the doubt, though. Perhaps he never would. And from that uncertainty, all the others had grown. And the drinking. Perhaps the drinking most of all. The churchyard mistake had certainly been through booze.

And all the others, before. At least that had stopped, after the latest scare. Odd how real fear made him abandon alcohol. Survival again, she supposed.

'How long have you been awake?

She turned at his question, discarding the charade of sleep.

'Quite a while. You?'

'Quite a while.'

'I still wish you wouldn't go.'

'I've got to.'

'They couldn't find us now.'

He didn't reply and she demanded urgently, 'Could they?'

'If I don't meet Rupert Willoughby, he might contact the department,' he said. 'Don't forget how closely his father involved him ... he wouldn't have the hesitation of anyone else. And if he were to telephone them, he'd give them the lead they need.'

'You said it was safe here,' she accused him. 'We moved back the same day, for heaven's sake.'

'I overlooked it,' he admitted. Like so many other things, he thought.

'You could be exposing yourself completely,' she warned, frowning at the repetition of a previous argument.

'I'll be careful,' he said. 'Very careful.'

'Will you bother about the money?'

'I don't know.'

So he *did* think he had been identified. If she hadn't kept on about quitting England completely, they wouldn't have gone back for the confounded money, she thought bitterly. The fact that she was a rich woman had always been a barrier between them.

Frightened that he might detect her tears in the growing half-light, Edith turned towards the window. Lake Zürich was already visible, dull and flat like a thrown-away silver dish.

'What happens if he *has* contacted them?' she asked, bringing the fear into the open. 'It would be a trap.'

Again there was a pause. Then he said: 'I won't know. Not until I get there.'

They'd move on, she knew. Again. Away from the hideout where she felt most safe, just five minutes' walk from the Swiss Bank Corporation building in the Paradeplatz where her money was held in its numbered account, together with the false passports and forged documents, another identity to be donned, like new clothes, if that under which they had existed for the past two years were discovered because of that bloody graveyard idiocy.

Move on to where? At least not back to the small, greasy apartment in the Pigalle area of Paris, she thought gratefully; smelly and anonymous rooms among the no-questions-asked hotels in which the transient workers from North Africa and Turkey lived out their frightened existence, without the proper entry or work permits. So where? God knows.

'I wish you hadn't done it, Charlie.'

'I've apologised, haven't I? Don't you think I regret it, every bit as much as you?'

She held back the response, recognising the defiance in his voice. She *wouldn't* argue, she determined. There was no purpose in holding an inquest. She gnawed at the inside of her cheek, caught by the word. Inquests were for people who had died. Usually violently.

'I'll go by myself, of course,' he said.

'Of course,' she agreed. Quickly, the feeling clogging her voice, Edith added: 'Be careful.'

He laughed.

'I'm a survivor, remember?'

'I'm very frightened, Charlie. It's different now. You're completely on your own. And everything seems to be going wrong.'

'That's how I've always been, on my own.'

She moved her head, a rustling gesture of rejection against the pillow.

'I love you, Charlie,' she said. 'I couldn't bear to live without you.'

'You won't have to.'

'I wish I could believe that.'

She waited for the reassurance to be repeated, but Charlie said nothing. The tears she had so far managed to hold back began feeling their way across her face and she turned farther towards the window, away from him.

'You haven't said you loved me for a long time,' he remarked and she started crying even more.

In Moscow, the British ambassador, Sir Robert Black, accepted the sheaf of papers from the Soviet Minister of Culture and affixed his signature. The signing of the outline agreement completed, both men rose from the table. Immediately the waiters approached with the trays of drinks for the regulation toasts. Despite the regeneration of the British economy, it was sherry, not champagne. The Russian, Boris Navetsky, hesitated, looking disdainfully at the amber liquid. Bloody mean, he thought.

'My country is eagerly looking forward to the exhibition,' said the ambassador.

Navetsky nodded.

'A pity, perhaps,' ventured the Briton, 'that it was not possible for the actual Romanov jewellery to be displayed.'

'It is only the Fabergé replicas that have ever been allowed to leave the country on exhibition,' Navetsky reminded him stiffly. He'd refuse a second drink, he decided.

'Surely you don't imagine my country would expose such works of art to any risk?' said the ambassador.

'Of course not,' Navetsky assured him.

In London, a report on the exhibition of the Russian royal jewellery was despatched, as a matter of routine, from the Foreign Office to Wilberforce. It was to be several days before he read it.

The protection would never be necessary, Johnny Packer

knew. But like Herbie Pie had said, he was a craftsman. And craftsmen always did things properly. So at the back of the shed, where the more volatile explosives were stored, Johnny had constructed a double-thickness brick wall, to cushion any accidental blast. Each was housed in its carefully partitioned section, with metal sheets forming an inner lining. The P-4 plastic, the easiest and least dangerous to use, was most readily to hand. Then the cordite, which he disliked because of the difficulty of control in certain circumstances. And in front of it all, the sacks of sodium chlorate, to be mixed with the sugar in the kitchen if the sudden need arose. Which he hoped it wouldn't. Sodium chlorate and sugar was all right for the killers of Belfast, but Johnny Packer was a craftsman.

Away from the explosive material but still within the reinforced area the fuses and detonators were packed carefully into their boxes and in a third case were the clocks and pressure mechanisms.

He locked the shed and began walking round to the house. With equipment like that, there wasn't an explosive device he couldn't construct, decided Johnny. But when? Six weeks and there'd been nothing. It was a test, Johnny knew. The trade ... the real, no-fucking-about trade ... had to be sure he'd learned his lesson. Trouble was, the only way to prove that was to do a job. And without help, how the hell was he going to do that?

EIGHT

Charlie had allowed himself three days before the London meeting. The first two had been taken up travelling to England by as confused a route as possible, going by train from Zürich to Lyons, from there to Paris, backtracking to Auxerre and then returning to Paris to catch the night sleeper to Victoria.

The remaining day had been devoted entirely to watching Rupert Willoughby, following him from his house off Sloane Street to his City office, occupying the secluded table at Sweetings during the man's business lunch, checking his firm to uncover any possible links to dummy or cover companies the names and addresses of which he might have recognised and then, finally, trailing him in his trendy, smoked-glass mini back from the City to Knightsbridge in the evening. Just like old times, reflected Charlie, welcoming the activity.

It would have needed a team of men to have established absolutely that the man was not under deep surveillance, Charlie accepted. And as Edith had warned, now he was completely on his own.

And so he would always be now, he reflected, content with the protection of the rush-hour crowd in the middle of which he spilled from the Bank underground station on the morning of the appointment.

'So far, so good,' he assured himself.

'Yes,' agreed a commuter beside him. 'Much better this morning, wasn't it? Extra trains at London Bridge, you know.'

'About time,' answered Charlie. He'd have to control the habit, he decided. It was embarrassing.

The office of the Lloyd's underwriters of which, from enquiries he'd already made through the Company Register, Charlie knew Willoughby to be the senior partner, was off Leadenhall Street, high in a converted block with a view of the Bank of England.

Willoughby was already standing when Charlie entered the spacious, oak-panelled office. Immediately he came forward, hands held out like that Sunday in the churchyard. Remarkably like his father, decided Charlie. Even more so than he had realised from their initial encounter.

'At last,' greeted the underwriter, leading Charlie to a leather, button-backed chair immediately alongside the desk.

'At last?'

Willoughby smiled at the quickness of the question, looking down at the man. Thinning, strawish hair, perhaps a hint of blood pressure or even alcohol from the slight purpling around the face and nose and a hunched, maybe apprehensive way of sitting. A very ordinary sort of man; the 8 a.m. traveller on every bus and train. Which proved, decided Willoughby, how deceptive appearances could be.

'I always hoped you would make contact,' he said. 'If you could, that was. My father did, too.'

Very direct, assessed Charlie. Almost as if the man had some knowledge of what had happened.

'I've cancelled everything for today,' said Willoughby. 'There'll be no interruptions.'

Charlie remained silent, sitting forward in the chair. How could Willoughby know? It was impossible. Unless he were involved in the pursuit. And if he were involved, then he wouldn't be so direct, arousing suspicion. It was a circle of doubt, Charlie recognised, without a beginning or an end.

'So we finally meet,' said Willoughby again, as if he couldn't believe it.

'There was a previous occasion,' Charlie reminded him. Willoughby had been at Cambridge, Charlie recalled. Sir Archibald had brought him into the Whitehall office on his way for his first visit to the House of Commons. The boy had acne and seemed disappointed nobody carried a gun.

'I'm sorry,' apologised Willoughby. 'I don't remember meeting you with my father. But he didn't take me into the office very often.'

'No,' agreed Charlie.

'Do you know,' continued Willoughby, leaning back in his chair and looking away from Charlie, 'in the end those bastards Cuthbertson and Wilberforce actually tried to use something as ridiculous as that against him.'

'What?' demanded Charlie, very attentive. The continued openness was disconcerting; almost the professional use of honesty that he had employed to gain a person's confidence.

43

'His taking me into the office,' explained the underwriter. 'Claimed it was a breach of security.'

Charlie felt the tension recede. It would be wrong to formulate impressions too soon. But perhaps it hadn't been a mistake to come, after all.

'It's the sort of thing they would have done,' accepted Charlie. And been right, he thought honestly. But Sir Archibald had always made his own rules; that was one of the reasons why he and Charlie had established such a rapport. And why, in the end, Cuthbertson and Wilberforce had manoeuvred his replacement.

'You realise he committed suicide, don't you?' said Willoughby.

Charlie shook his head.

'No,' he said. 'I didn't. I was away when he died. It was never directly mentioned, but I inferred it was natural causes ...'

Charlie paused.

'Well ...' he started again, but Willoughby talked over him.

'Cirrhosis of the liver?' anticipated the man. 'Yes, that too. They made him into an alcoholic by the way they treated him. And when he realised what had happened to him, he hoarded some barbiturates and took the whole lot with a bottle of whisky.'

'I'm sorry,' Charlie began, then stopped, irritated by the emptiness of the expression. But he *was* sorry, he thought. There were few people to whom he had ever been close. And Sir Archibald had been one of them.

'There was a note,' continued Willoughby, appearing unaware of Charlie's attempt at sympathy. 'Several, in fact. The one he left for the police put the fear of Christ up everyone. Spelled everything out ... not just what shits Cuthbertson and Wilberforce were in the way they got him fired, but the mistakes they had made as well. He did it quite deliberately because he believed that if they weren't moved, they'd make a major, serious blunder.'

His feelings, remembered Charlie.

44

'The department took the whole thing over,' continued Willoughby. 'They have the power, apparently, under the Official Secrets Act. Allows them to do practically anything, to protect the national interest. Squashed the inquest, everything. That's how the natural causes account got spread about.'

Sir Archibald's death could only have been a matter of weeks before he had exposed their stupidity and got them captured in Vienna by the Russian commandos, Charlie calculated. What, he wondered, had happened to Cuthbertson? Back where he belonged, probably, fighting long forgotten battles over the brandy and cigars at Boodles. Wilberforce would have survived, he guessed. Wilberforce, with his poofy socks and shirts and that daft habit of breaking pipes into little pieces. Always had been a sneaky bugger, even under Sir Archibald's control. Yes, he would certainly have hung on, shifting all the blame on to Cuthbertson. Would he still be the second-in-command? Or had he finally got the Directorship for which he had schemed for so long? Always an ambitious man: but without the ability to go with it. If he had remained, then the danger of which Sir Archibald had warned still existed.

'He asked me to tell you the truth, if ever you contacted me,' said Willoughby.

'I don't . . .' frowned Charlie.

'I told you he wrote several letters. To avoid them being seized by the police, he posted them, on the night he killed himself. He really planned it very carefully. The one to me talked about his fears for the department . . . he felt very strongly about it, after all those years, and didn't want it destroyed because incapable men had managed to reach positions of power. And another was devoted almost entirely to you.'

'Oh.'

'He told you you'd visited him . . . just before going away to do something about which you were frightened.'

So he'd realised it, thought Charlie. He'd imagined Sir Archibald too drunk that day he had gone down to Rye and sat in the darkened room and felt the sadness lump in his throat at the collapse of the old man.

'He appreciated it very much ... the fact that you regarded him as a friend.'

It was true, reflected Charlie. That was always how he'd thought of the man under whom he had spent all his operational life.

'He often talked about you when ... when he was Director and we were living together, in London. Boasted about you, in fact. Said you were the best operative he had ever created ... that there was practically nothing you couldn't do ...'

The man's forthrightness was not assumed, decided Charlie, unembarrassed at the flattery. Willoughby would have made a mistake by now, had he had to force the effect. 'There were times when I was almost jealous of you.' Willoughby added.

'I don't think he'd be very proud now,' said Charlie, regretting the admission as he spoke. Carelessness again.

Willougby raised his hands in a halting movement.

'I don't think I should know,' he said, quickly. He paused, then added bluntly: 'The guilt was pretty obvious in the cemetery.'

Justified criticism, accepted Charlie. He wouldn't have stood a chance if the graveyard had been covered that day.

'I've known for a long time they've been looking for you,' announced Willoughby.

Charlie came forward on his seat again and Willoughby tried to reduce the sudden awkwardness by smiling and leaning back in his own chair.

'You've no need to be concerned,' he said. He dropped the smile, reinforcing the assurance.

'How?' asked Charlie. His feet were beneath the chair, ready to take the weight when he jerked up.

'They remembered the relationship between you and my father,' recounted Willoughby. 'I had several visits from their people, about four months after he died ...'

'They would have asked you to have told them, if ever I

made contact with you,' predicted Charlie, the apprehension growing.

'That's right,' agreed Willoughby. 'They did.'

'Well?' Charlie demanded. He'd buggered it, he thought immediately. Edith had been right: he was wrong again.

'Charlie,' said Willoughby, coming forward again so that there was less than a yard between them. 'They reduced my father into a shambling, disgusting old drunk who went to sleep every night puddled in his own urine. And then, effectively, they killed him. I don't know what you did, but I know it hurt. Is it likely I'm going to turn in someone who did what I'd have given my eye-teeth to have done?'

Charlie was hunched in the chair, still uncertain.

'It's been five weeks since your telephone call,' Willoughby reminded him, realising Charlie's doubt. He waved his hand towards the window.

'In five weeks,' said the underwriter, 'they would have made plans that guaranteed that once inside this office you'd never be able to get out again. Go on, look out of the window. By now the roads would have been sealed and all the traffic halted.'

Willoughby was right, Charlie realised. He got up, going behind the other man's chair. Far below, the street was thronged with people and cars.

'The outer office would have been cleared, too,' invited the underwriter.

Without replying, Charlie opened the door. The secretary who had greeted him looked up, enquiringly, then smiled.

'Satisfied?' asked Willoughby.

Charlie nodded.

'Tell me something,' said Willoughby, in sudden curiosity. 'What would you have done if it had been a trap?'

'Probably tried to kill you,' said Charlie. And more than likely failed, he added to himself, remembering his hesitation at personal violence in the cemetery.

Willoughby pulled his lips over his teeth, a nervous gesture.

'What good would that have done, if you'd been bottled up here?'

'Kept me alive,' suggested Charlie. 'They couldn't have eliminated me, if I'd committed a public murder.'

Why, wondered Charlie, was he talking like this? It was ridiculous. He waited for the other man to laugh at him.

Willoughby remained blank-faced.

'And do they want to eliminate you?'

'I would imagine so.'

Willoughby shook his head in distaste.

'God, it's obscene,' he said.

Charlie frowned. That wasn't a sincere remark, he judged. The man still thought of it as he had as a boy that day in the office, a sort of game for grown-ups.

'Consider it,' Willoughby went on. 'Two men, sitting here in the middle of London, calmly using words like eliminate instead of planned, premeditated murder.'

'Yes,' agreed Charlie. 'Sometimes it has to happen. Though not as much as you might think ...'

He looked at the other man, to see if he were appreciating the words.

' ... thank God,' he concluded.

'That was one thing about the service over which my father could never lose his disgust,' recalled Willoughby. 'He talked to me a great deal ...'

He smiled over the hesitation. 'Cuthbertson and Wilberforce would say too much – another breach of security. My father believed very strongly in what he did ... the need for such a department. But he was always horrified that people occasionally had to die.'

'I know,' said Charlie. The remaining doubts were being swept away by the reminiscence. Willoughby would have had to be very close to his father – as close as he had been to him in the department – to know so well the old man's feelings.

Willoughby sighed, shedding the past.

'And now I know about you,' he said, gravely. 'Whether I wanted to or not.'

48

'Only their possible verdict,' qualified Charlie. 'Not the cause.'

'It must have been serious?'

'It was.'

For a moment, neither spoke. Then Willoughby said: 'My father often remarked about your honesty. Considered it unusual, in a business so involved in deceit.'

'You seem to have the same tendency.'

'My father preferred it.'

'Yes,' remembered Charlie. 'He did.'

It was strange, thought Charlie, what effect the old man had had upon both of them.

The intercom burped and Willoughby nodded briefly into the receiver, smiling up at Charlie when he replaced the earpiece.

'From your reaction in the cemetery, I thought you'd prefer lunch here, in the seclusion of the office,' he said. 'Now I'm sure you would.'

Charlie detected movement behind him and turned to see two waiters setting up a gatelegged table. There were oysters, duck in aspic, cheese, chablis and port. Underwriters lived well, he thought.

Willoughby waited until they had seated themselves at the table and begun to eat before he spoke again.

'I must satisfy myself about one thing, Charlie,' he said.

'What?'

'Whatever you did . . . was it illegal?'

Charlie examined the question. There couldn't be a completely honest answer, he decided.

'Nothing for which I would appear in any English court of law,' he said. 'I was just trying to achieve, although in a different way, the sort of changes that your father believed necessary.'

And survive, he thought.

Willoughby smiled.

'Then you've nothing to fear from me,' he said. 'The opposite in fact.'

'Opposite?'

'In the letter,' explained Willougby, 'the one in which he mentioned you so much, my father said he thought they were trying to do to you what they had done to him. He asked that if the opportunity or necessity arose that I should help you in any way I could.'

Charlie finished the oysters and sat fingering his glass, staring down into the wine he had scarcely touched. Trying to do to him what they'd done to Sir Archibald; certainly the drinking had become bad. He'd never considered suicide, though. And didn't think he ever would.

'You've already helped,' he said, 'by saying nothing.'

'There was something else,' continued the underwriter.

'What?'

'My father was a very rich man,' said Willoughby. 'Even after the setlement of the estate and the payment in full of death duties, there was still over three-quarters of a million pounds. He left you £50,000.'

'Good God!'

Willoughby laughed openly at the astonishment.

Charlie sat shaking his head. Three years ago, he reflected, he was saving the taxi fares from the Wormwood Scrubs debriefings with Alexei Berenkov by walking in the rain with holes in his shoes. Now he had more money than he knew what to do with. Why then, he wondered, did he feel so bloody miserable?

'I've had it for two years on long-term deposit at fourteen per cent,' added Willoughby. 'It'll have increased by quite a few thousand.'

'I don't really need it,' shrugged Charlie.

'It's legally yours,' said Willoughby.

And fairly his, added Charlie. Better even than the American money. He had more than Edith now. The thought lodged in his mind, to become an idea.

The meal over, Willoughby poured the port and leaned back in his chair.

'Why did you go to the cemetery, Charlie?' he asked. 'Surely, it was a dangerous thing to do?'

Charlie nodded.

'Absolutely insane,' he agreed.

Willoughby waited.

'I'd drunk too much,' Charlie admitted. 'It was becoming a habit. And I had intended it to be my last visit to England. So I wanted to make just one visit.'

'They *did* watch the grave,' offered Willoughby.

Charlie's eyes came up, questioningly.

'Must have been for almost six months,' expanded the underwriter. 'I go there about twice a month ... learned to recognise them, in the end. They were quite obvious, even to an amateur like me ...'

So he'd been lucky, decided Charlie. Bloody lucky.

'It wasn't just drink,' Charlie tried to explain. 'I'd always wanted to ... just couldn't take the risk, earlier ...'

He stopped, looking at Willoughby in sudden realisation.

'I came here to guarantee my own safety,' he said. 'You know, of course, that I could have compromised you ...'

There was no artifice in the gesture of dismissal, assessed Charlie. The underwriter definitely regarded it as a game for adults, he decided. But then, how would any outsider regard it otherwise?

'My distaste for them, Charlie, is far greater than yours. I loved my father.' Willoughby spoke without any embarrassment.

'I think we both did.'

'Are we going to meet again?' asked Willoughby.

Charlie sat, considering the question. For two years, he thought, he and Edith had been imprisoned, bound together in a bizarre form of solitary confinement by the knowledge of what he had done, able to trust no one. Being able to talk, comparatively freely, to Willoughby, was like having the dungeon door thrown open.

'It would hardly be fair to you,' said Charlie.

'You know how I feel about that.'

The unexpected inheritance intruded into his mind again, the ill-formed idea hardening. He'd got away from the cemetery. And Willoughby was sincere. He was safe. So now he had to do something to fill the vacuum that had been destroying him. The inheritance and Willoughby's occupation presented an opportunity from which he couldn't turn away. It would mean leaving a reserve of money in the Brighton bank, but he'd only agreed to move it because of Edith's insistence. She'd understand why he'd changed his mind: be glad he'd found something to interest him.

He cleared his throat. Willoughby could always reject it, he decided. And should do, if he had any sense. He was using the other man, Charlie realised. Just as he'd used Günther Bayer for the ambushed crossing. It didn't lessen the guilt to admit to himself that he was sometimes a shit, Charlie decided.

'I'm thinking of asking you to do something that might offend you,' he warned. 'Professionally, I mean.'

'What?'

The question was immediate, without the gap that would have indicated reluctance. The man thought he was being invited to play.

'The money your father left me ... the money I don't really need.'

'What about it?'

'Use it for me.'

'Use it?'

Charlie nodded.

'Part of the problem, the drinking I mean, was the absolute boredom,' he confessed. 'For almost two years, I've done nothing. Atrophied, almost. Can't I invest that money ... more, if it's not enough, through you?'

Willoughby poured himself some more port.

'There couldn't be anything in writing,' he said, thinking aloud.

'That doesn't worry me.'

Willoughby looked up, smiling at the trust.

'A very silent Lloyd's underwriter,' he identified. 'Breaking every rule in the profession.'

'So I'd be embarrassing you,' said Charlie.

Willoughby made an uncaring motion with his hand.

'I can't see how,' he said. 'The money would be in my name ... nothing traceable to you ... I was executor of my father's estate, so it can be transferred without any problem.'

Again the underwriter smiled.

'And it would create the need for us to meet from time to time, wouldn't it?' he said presciently.

'Yes,' admitted Charlie. He waited several moments, then added: 'I'm asking you to take a very big risk.'

'I know,' said Willoughby.

'Greater than I've really any right to ask, despite the request of your father.'

'Yes.'

'It would be right for you to refuse ... sensible to do so, in fact,' advised Charlie.

'Yes, it would,' said Willoughby. After a moment's pause, he added: 'But we both know I won't refuse, don't we?'

Yes, thought Charlie.

The underwriter stood, proffering his hand.

'This is the only way we'll have of binding the agreement,' he said.

'It's sufficient for me,' said Charlie, shaking the offered hand.

'Underwriting is sometimes dangerous,' warned Willoughby.

'Any more dangerous than what I've done so far?'

Willoughby laughed at the sarcasm.

'Sorry,' he said. 'I live a normal life and it's easy to forget.'

'Perhaps,' said Charlie, 'going to the cemetery wasn't the mistake I believed it might be.'

'No,' reflected Willoughby. 'I don't think it was.'

The ambassador turned away from the window and its view of the Moscow skyline, smeared grey by the sleeting rain. Next week, when it snowed, Moscow would look beautiful again, he thought.

Idly, Sir Robert picked up the inventory that had arrived

that morning from the Hermitage in Leningrad, comparing it to the list from the Moscow Armoury. The Russians were making available far less of the regalia than he had expected from the agreement he had signed with the Minister of Culture, he saw. Still, at least they were letting some out. He supposed he should be grateful for that.

In London, a man whose hatred of Charlie Muffin was absolute sat in an office adjoining that of George Wilberforce, carefully examining the files obtained through the combined but unsuspecting channels of the Special Branch, Scotland Yard records, the Inland Revenue and the Bank of England and Clearing Houses security sections. A vivid scar disfigured the left side of his face and as he worked his fingers kept straying to it, an habitual movement.

Tonight he was concentrating upon the Special Branch and Scotland Yard dossiers and after two hours one folder remained for detailed consideration on the left of the desk.

'John Packer,' he identified, slowly, opening the cover.

He read for a further hour, then pushed it away.

'From now on,' he said, staring down at the official police photographs, 'it's the big time for you, John Packer ...'

He paused.

' ... for a while, anyway,' he added.

NINE

Edith looked away from the view from the Baur au Lac balcony, coming back to her husband. It had been a long time, she thought, since she had see him as relaxed and as happy as this. Almost two years, in fact. She'd never know him completely, she accepted. He was a strange man.

'You're fun again, Charlie,' she said gratefully.

He responded seriously to the remark.

'I'm sorry,' he said.

'It's been ages,' she said.

'It'll be better now,' he promised.

'It's a lot of money,' she protested cautiously, reverting to the conversation in which they'd been engaged throughout the dinner.

'Two hundred thousand, added to what Sir Archibald left me,' recounted Charlie. 'Still less than half of what I've got. And that's not an unusual amount for underwriters to deposit. To be admitted simply as a member of Lloyd's needs assets of £75,000.'

He saw it as even greater independence from her money, she realised. Not moving the remainder from the Brighton bank worried her.

'You're not a normal underwriter. I'm amazed the man agreed.'

'So am I,' admitted Charlie. 'He shouldn't have done.'

'You're quite sure it's safe?' she asked, a frequent question since he had returned from London three weeks earlier.

Charlie sighed patiently.

'I've checked the firm thoroughly,' he reminded her. 'There's no trace with any of the standby companies the department use for links with outside businesses. And for three days after I made the arrangement with Rupert Willoughby I watched him, from morning to night. There was no contact whatsoever.'

'You still can't be one hundred per cent sure.'

'Ninety-nine is good enough.'

'It used not to be.'

Charlie frowned at her concern.

'Edith,' he lectured her, 'it's now over six weeks since the cemetery ... almost a month since I went to London, by an appointment they would have known about had he been in any way connected with them. And here we are having a pleasant dinner in one of the best restaurants in Zürich. If Rupert Willoughby weren't genuine, then I wouldn't be alive. We both know that.'

She nodded, in reluctant agreement. His involvement

55

with Willoughby would provide the interest he had lacked, she decided. And it was wonderful to see him laugh again.

'I suppose you're right,' she said.

'I always have been.'

That was another thing that had been absent for too long, Charlie's confidence. It had been one of the first things to attract her, she remembered. It had been at a party at the Paris embassy, where Charlie had been on secondment and she had been the guest of the ambassador. The diplomat had apologised for Charlie afterwards, she recalled. Described him as an upstart. When she'd told Charlie, he'd nodded quite seriously and said 'bloody right': and two weeks later established that the ambassador's mistress had links with Soviet intelligence.

'What are you smiling about?' asked Charlie.

'Just thinking,' said Edith.

'What about?'

'You.'

He smiled back at her.

'It's going to be all right, Edith,' he promised.

'Tell me something, Charlie,' she said, leaning over the table to enforce the question. 'Honestly, I mean.'

'What?'

'You regret it, don't you?'

He took his time over the answer.

'Some things,' he admitted. 'People died, which is always wrong. But I'm not sorry I exposed Cuthbertson and his band of idiots.'

He stopped, smiling sadly.

'I tried to do it and Sir Archibald tried to do it,' he recalled. 'And I wouldn't mind betting that people like Wilberforce have still clung on. Bureaucracy is a comfort blanket to people like that.'

'The killing wasn't your fault,' she said.

'Some was,' he insisted. Günther Bayer had had a fiancée in West Berlin, he remembered. Gretel. She'd been preparing a celebration dinner on the night of the crossing and Günther had wanted him to go.

'Not all.'

'But for me, it wouldn't have happened.'

'No one would be feeling regrets if you'd died,' she said. 'And God knows, they tried hard enough.'

'Only you,' he said.

'Yes,' she agreed, 'I'd still be regretting it.'

Did Charlie have the love for her that she felt for him? wondered Edith. She wished he'd tell her so, more often.

'And the money was a mistake,' he conceded. 'It was necessary, to make the Kalenin crossing seem absolutely genuine. But to take it was wrong ...'

Because it put a price on his betrayal, decided Edith. Money – his lack of it and her inheritance – had always been a problem for Charlie. He'd accepted the house beyond that which he could have afforded on his Grade IV salary. And the furnishing. But he had always adamantly refused any for his personal needs, keeping shoes until they were worn through and suits until they were shiny at the seat and elbows. He'd actually tried to change, in the early months after the Kalenin affair. He'd bought Yves St Laurent and Gucci and looked as comfortable as Cinderella at five minutes to midnight. The seat and elbows weren't shiny, but the suit still came from a department store. And the shoes were still Hush Puppies, even though they weren't down at heel any more. Charlie would always be the sort of person to wear a string vest with a see-through shirt, she thought fondly.

'Let's stop living in the past,' she said.

He nodded, brightening.

'Right,' he accepted. 'At last we've got something to consider in the future ... I'm going into high finance, Edith.'

She laughed with him, trying to match his enthusiasm. Please God, she thought, make it last. She hadn't liked Charlie Muffin very much in the last two years.

'John Packer?'

The safebreaker looked up from his drink, gazing steadily at the man standing at the other side of the table.

'Yes,' continued the man, as if satisfying some private question. 'You're John Packer.'

Packer sat back, waiting. The man pulled out a chair and sat down, smiling. Smart, decided Packer. But not flash. Good voice; air of breeding, too, so he could make everyone else feel a turd. Confidence trickster, maybe. Nasty scar on his face. Perhaps a job had gone wrong.

'What do you want?' asked Packer.

'Want?' echoed the man, as if it were an amusing demand. 'I want to put you into the major league, John Packer.'

TEN

George Wilberforce sat easily at his desk, moving a pipe between his long fingers, letting everyone else settle in the Whitehall office. They'd all come to him, he thought. And that was how it was going to be, until the end of the operation. He was going to be in command.

'We're ready to move against Charlie Muffin,' he announced. 'Tonight.'

'Still think it's a waste of time,' said Ruttgers defiantly.

'Not if it makes Charlie Muffin suffer.'

Everyone turned to the speaker, one of the two men whom Wilberforce had accepted for the final planning session. It had taken almost a year for Brian Snare to recover physically from his Moscow imprisonment, Wilberforce remembered. He looked at the man. Perhaps, in other ways, he never would. Snare's hand had gone automatically to the jagged, star-shaped scar where the skin had burst, rather than been cut, on the left side of his face. A warder's boot in Lubyanka had caused that, Wilberforce knew. But at least he was still alive. Douglas Harrison had been shot down by East German Grenzschutztruppen.

Wilberforce moved to speak, then paused, halted by a sudden thought. It had been Snare and Harrison, following Cuthbertson's instructions, who had actually set Charlie Muffin up for sacrifice in East Berlin. And Charlie's retribution had been planned as carefully as that which he himself was now evolving to destroy the man, decided Wilberforce. In many ways, he thought, he and Charlie were very similar. He was just a little cleverer, determined the Director. As he was going to prove.

'It would be a mistake to let personal feelings overly affect our judgment on this,' warned the other newcomer. William Braley had been the C.I.A. Resident in the American embassy in Moscow specially appointed to work with Charlie on the last stages of Kalenin's supposed crossing. Few people knew Charlie better, which was why Braley was being included in the discussion.

Reminded of the association, Wilberforce said: 'Do you think there's any undue risk in what has been proposed?'

The man squinted nervously at the direct question. Braley was a man fattened by a glandular malfunction and given to asthma in moments of tension. Predictably, his breathing became jerky and he wondered if he would be able to use his inhaler.

'There's always a danger with Charlie Muffin,' he pointed out. 'We should never forget that.'

'But can he react any other way than that which we expect?'

Again Braley delayed replying, feeling his chest tighten further.

'No,' he said at last. 'I've thought about it, putting myself in his place. And I don't think he can.'

Wilberforce smiled, turning to the others in the room, patting as he did so the thick file that lay before him on the desk.

'You've all read the dossier,' he said. 'There hasn't been a moment since we picked him up at the cemetery when Charlie Muffin has not been under detailed surveillance.

59

There's not a thing we don't know about him. And we've planned against every eventuality.'

'He seems to have found a friend in Rupert Willoughby,' remarked Cuthbertson:

'For the moment, that doesn't affect what we are going to do,' said Wilberforce. But it might, later on, he thought, remembering the report of the Russian exhibition. He was beginning to enjoy the idea of Charlie Muffin dancing in whatever direction he dictated; and if tonight went as he expected, that was all the man would be able to do from now on – perform as ordered.

'So we go ahead?' demanded Snare anxiously.

Wilberforce came back to the man who was going to be most dangerously involved in manipulating Charlie Muffin. He seemed desperate for them to agree, thought the Director. Which was out of character, for what he was being expected to do. But then, he'd suffered probably more than any of them. So his need for revenge was stronger.

'Well?' queried Wilberforce, taking the question to the Americans. He still had to give them the impression of consultation, he thought, even if it were really he who was making the decisions.

'You're still sure that what you propose will bring Charlie Muffin back to England?' said Onslow Smith.

'He won't be able to do anything else.'

'What if you're wrong?' said Ruttgers.

It was time, realised the British Director, to make concessions. Hardly a concession; if Charlie didn't respond as he expected, then it would have to be done anyway, despite the risk of any incriminating documents Charlie might have prepared.

'If Charlie Muffin isn't back in Brighton within three days,' said Wilberforce, 'then I agree he should be immediately killed.'

He smiled, deciding to extend the offer.

'Why not send an assassination squad to Switzerland, just in case?' he suggested. 'That way there would be absolutely no risk.'

60

Onslow Smith shrugged, an almost embarrassed gesture. 'We already have,' he admitted.

'And I'm going there tonight,' added Ruttgers, smiling to expose his yellow teeth.

Wilberforce frowned. Ruttgers was determined to be present when it happened, he thought. And the unexpected independence of Onslow was irritating.

'So we go ahead,' he announced.

ELEVEN

A professional, judged Johnny Packer. A bloody good professional, too. The knowledge tightened inside him, a comforting feeling. Which meant he was regarded in the same way. So this was going to be proof. No one would doubt him, after this.

'Drill.'

Johnny looked up at the order. The other man was breathing heavily through the exertion of crawling along the confined space and the jagged, star-shaped scar on the left side of his face had reddened into an ugly blotch. Appearing suddenly aware of the disfigurement, he put his hand up, covering it. He often made the gesture, Johnny realised. When they'd got to know each other better, he'd have to ask him how it had happened. They would become friends in time, he hoped. Proper friends.

Johnny passed the tool along the narrow air conditioning duct to the other man, wondering what his real name was. If he hadn't been such an obvious expert, Johnny would have sniggered at the man's insistence on Brown. But he hadn't. It wouldn't have been right. He wasn't the sort of person you laughed at. Or with, even. If he wanted to play around with names, that was all right with Johnny. Another indication of how good he was, really; neither knew the other, so there couldn't be any risk of grassing if one were caught. Not quite true, corrected the safebreaker. The other man knew his name. And his record. And that he'd only been out for four months. The knowledge didn't disturb Johnny. He regarded it as another indication of professionalism.

The drill, rubber-cushioned, began eating into the ducting at the spot the other man had selected, working from a set of draughtsman's plans. Johnny leaned against the cold metal, experiencing another surge of admiration. Plans not just of the adjoining buildings and central heating and air conditioning systems, but every alarm installation in the place. And all the tools they were likely to need, brand new and bought with cash, one at each town along the south coast in an undetectable preparation that had taken over a week. They'd spent at least £4,000, guessed Johnny. He'd even queried the figure.

The man had smiled and said: 'You've got to speculate to accumulate,' and made it sound original.

Bloody professional.

'Cutters.'

The snips went along the narrow passageway and Snare enlarged the hole, then drilled into the mortar. Johnny started back at the sudden eruption of dust, lacking the protection of the face mask that Snare had put on.

'Vacuum.'

The more subdued whine of the cleaner came as a relief after the harsher bite of the drill.

'There!'

Johnny strained forward, narrowing his eyes at the brightness of the extension lamp which Snare had erected over the hole he had begun to mark. The blue and green wires of the alarm system embedded into the concrete stood out like veins in an old man's hand.

Snare reached back and Johnny gave him the bypass leads. Snare clamped them at either end of the exposed alarms, scraping his way through the plastic covering with a surgeon's scalpel, then cut through the middle of the wire. They had made long connections, maybe five feet, giving themselves room for a big entry hole. Snare taped the surplus wire against the metal sides of the ducting so there would be no risk of dislodging it, and then began drilling again, enlarging the hole.

It took almost an hour, with two stops to vacuum away the debris before Snare stopped.

'Enough,' he announced. He turned, gesturing Johnny back. Dutifully, the safebreaker turned and crawled along the shaft until he reached their carefully reinforced entry point, then dropped down into the basement of the building adjoining the bank in Brighton's North Street.

'What's the matter?' he asked worriedly, as the other man dropped through immediately behind him.

'Coffee break,' announced Snare.

He went to one of the four haversacks they'd brought in, took out a Thermos and poured the drinks. His hands were shaking, Johnny realised, embarrassed, as he cupped the plastic beaker to his lips. And the heat of the drink was making the surgical gloves he wore wet and sticky.

'We're thirty minutes ahead of schedule,' he said.

'You mustn't worry about time.'

Johnny smiled, knowing the other man had seen his nervousness.

'It's not yet midnight. Tomorrow's Sunday, so you've got all the time in the world,' the man assured him.

Johnny nodded.

'Shan't need it,' he said, trying to sound confident. 'Couple of hours and there won't be a lock still in place.'

Snare smiled tolerantly, hand up to his scarred face. It wasn't proving as difficult as he had feared, he decided, feeling the well-concealed apprehension ebbing away. He found a strange comfort in having so many plans to work from: it was always easier, having properly prepared diagrams to follow.

'Just don't worry,' he advised the other man.

It was ten minutes before they went back into the air conditioning system and this time Johnny led, hauling the light with him. There was a hole about three feet in diameter cut into the bank wall. Careful to avoid the clamped arms, Johnny eased through, wedging the light on top of a filing cabinet.

'Storeroom,' Snare identified it, a fresh set of plans in his hand now. He felt out for a switch and the neon light flickered into life. Filing cabinets lined the walls and in one corner files were heaped, one on top of the other.

They went out of the room, Johnny still in front.

'Manager's office first,' instructed Snare.

The door at the top of the steps was secured from the far side, but by squinting through Johnny saw the key was still in the lock.

'Easy,' he smiled, looking for some reaction. Snare gazed back, unimpressed.

From the attaché case, new like everything else, Johnny took the long-spined dentist's pliers, poked through to grip the key shank and unlocked the door.

On the main floor of the bank they relied upon shielded torches, moving slowly between furniture towards the office which Snare had designated. That, too, was locked and this time the key was missing. Johnny smeared thick grease on to a sliver of plastic, pushed it into the lock and then gently twisted, as if it were a key. He withdrew it and the tumbler edges were imprinted clearly into the grease. He lay the coated plastic along a matching piece of metal, plugged a dentist's electric drill into a table lamp socket and within five minutes had cut the basic shape of the key from the impression he had made. It took a further ten minutes to file away the mistakes and open the door. As he moved to do so, Snare touched his shoulder, pushing the light around the surround. The alarm breaker was near the top of the jamb. They used another bypass, magnetised this time, putting wedges either side of the door so that it wouldn't swing and pull the wire free.

'The first safe,' said Snare.

'Standard Chubb.'

'Difficult?'

'Course it's difficult.'

'But not impossible?'

'Not impossible,' said Johnny.

He worked with a stethoscope, hearing the tumblers into place. Twice, in his nervousness, he over-adjusted, missing the combination.

'What about the key?' asked Snare, reaching out to the second lock.

'Drill it out,' decided Johnny. 'Can't work the same trick as with the door.'

He used the dentist's drill again, first driving out the rivets and securing screws and then, when there was sufficient looseness in the lock to pull it back, revealing the securing arm, inserted the blade of the electric saw and cut through it.

Johnny pulled the door back and then stood away, for Snare to get to it. Files and documents were neatly stacked on the shelves and at the bottom there was a small cash box.

Snare worked through the documents in complete concentration. Anything he didn't want he replaced tidily within the file and then put the file back upon the shelf from which he'd removed it.

'Ah!'

Snare turned, smiling.

'Here it is.'

The man moved away from the safe with a sheaf of papers.

'What about the cash box?'

Snare turned to the safebreaker, the pain etched into his face.

'Let's leave them their tea money, shall we?'

Johnny trailed the man from the office, face burning with regret at his first mistake. At Snare's insistence, he relocked the manager's door, then went back down the stairs, turning off at the first landing towards the barred safety deposit room.

The opening was like a huge safe door, set into metal barriers within the protection of the wall. Johnny felt another jump of excitement. He'd done one before, he recognised. So it wouldn't be difficult; he'd pass the test.

He used the stethoscope again, more controlled this time, so he didn't over-adjust the combination control. After the third tumbler, he allowed himself the conceit, counting aloud as each combination clicked home.

'No alarms,' declared Snare, bent over another blueprint.

The man hadn't noticed the expertise, realised Johnny, annoyed. Irritably he pulled open the entrance to the vault.

The gates that formed the secondary barrier were ceiling to floor, protected by a wire alarm system and then by an electrified beam which triggered a signal when it was broken by any interruption between the 'eyes'. Snare bypassed the first as he had the other wired precautions, then placed immediately in front of the door two wire cages used in hospitals to keep the pressure of bedclothes off patients suffering from broken limbs. Securing holes had been bored in the frames and he quickly bolted them to the floor. The beam played unbroken beneath the cages. To get into the deposit room, they would have to step over but even if their feet hit the protection, the bolts prevented it sliding into the beam.

Johnny stooped before the lock, then shook his head.

'Have to blow it.'

Snare nodded, accepting the judgment.

From the attaché case, Johnny took his favourite, the P-4 plastic and a detonator, pressing it around the lock. Briefly in command now, he sent Snare to an office to get cushions and these he wired around the explosives, legs straddling the invalid hoops.

The explosion, decided Johnny, made up for the mistake over the petty cash box. He'd wedged the door, in case it swung too hard against the cages, but so well had he primed it that the caution wasn't necessary. The lock blew with a muffled, crackling sound, hardly displacing the cushions.

'Very good,' Snare praised him. The department's detailed training in use and construction of explosive devices

66

would have been more than sufficient, decided Snare. But then, the real purpose of Packer's involvement came later.

Johnny smiled, grateful for the remark.

Inside the safety deposit room, Johnny worked again from impressions, operating to Snare's quiet instructions from the list of box holders. They took only cash and jewellery. Documents were replaced and then the boxes locked again. Snare stood in the middle of the room, packing the cash into stiff-sided cases and the jewellery into a leather hold-all.

'What do you reckon?' demanded Johnny, unable to control the excited question. 'How much?'

The other man looked at him, as if he found the query curious.

'Maybe a million,' he said, casually.

It wasn't normal, thought Johnny, for someone to be as calm as this bugger was.

They worked for another hour, the only conversation Snare's commands to the other man. Suddenly, Snare said: 'Try 216.'

It took Johnny fifteen minutes to get the key right. He moved the lock, tugging at the deep metal tray as he did so and then stopped in amazement.

'Jesus!' he said softly.

Snare made no response, calmly reaching over his shoulder and extracting the dollars, banded together in tight bricks. He abandoned the suitcases, counting the money out on a small table in the corner of the room.

'Two hundred thousand,' he announced. 'And some insurance policies.'

Christ, he was cool, admired Johnny. Still not showing the slightest excitement. His own stomach was in turmoil and he knew he'd have diarrhoea in the morning.

Snare packed the money into a hold-all he kept separate from the containers in which he'd stored the rest of the property.

'What about the policies?' asked Johnny.

The other man hesitated, then laughed.

'Leave the policies,' he said. 'The bastard is going to need all the insurance he can get.'

There were no incriminating documents anywhere: Charlie Muffin had been too conceited. Always had been. So now there wasn't a thing he could do to prevent his own destruction.

Johnny frowned.

'You know him, then?'

Again the hand came up to the disfigurement.

'Oh yes,' said the man. 'I know him.'

It had been worth it, decided Snare. Every gut-churning minute had been worth it.

The Aeroflot freight carrier touched down precisely on schedule and taxied to the north side of London airport, where maximum security could be guaranteed. Ignoring the rain, the diplomats from the Russian embassy insisted on standing next to the ramp, ticking the numbered boxes against the manifest as they were unloaded on to the ground and then into armoured cars.

'These sort of jobs frighten the piss out of me,' said a Special Branch inspector, huddled in the doorway for protection.

His sergeant looked at him quizzically.

'It's only jewellery,' he said. 'And copies at that.'

'Fabergé copies,' corrected the inspector. 'Lose sight of one piece of this and our feet won't touch the bloody ground.'

TWELVE

Because two film actors and an M.P. were named among the victims, a single-column story on the bank robbery was even carried in the *Neue Zürcher Zeitung*, where Charlie read it first.

From the international news-stand in the foyer of the Dolder Hotel, he managed to buy that day's *Daily Telegraph* and *The Times*. Both led their front pages with it; the *Telegraph* even had a diagram, showing the thieves' entry. The work of complete professionals, a police spokesman was quoted as saying. Until all the safe deposit box-holders were contacted, no positive assessment could be made of the value.

'The bastards,' said Charlie. 'The cunning bastards.'

He paused on the Kurhausstrasse outside the hotel. He was trapped, he recognised objectively. In a way he'd never foreseen. He prolonged the hesitation, then made his way to a pavement café to consider it fully before going home to Edith. She'd panic, he knew. Especially so soon after the cemetery business. And panic was the last thing he could afford. Not any more. So what could he afford? Very little.

'Charlie,' he said. 'You've made a balls of it, like everything else. And now they've got you.'

The waiter who had served his coffee turned enquiringly and Charlie shook his head.

The involvement of the civil police – and the restrictions it would impose upon him – had been the one thing he had never envisaged, he realised. The one simple, obvious thing that took away his freedom to react in anything but a predictable way. So who was it? Wilberforce? He was devious enough. Or just bad luck, the chance-in-a-million he could never insure against? And why this way? To let him know he'd been found, and then watch him scrabbling for escape, like an animal in a trap of which they had the key? More than that, he decided. What then? He didn't know. He'd need more clues. And they'd be sure to prevent that.

'Never run,' he reminded himself. 'Basic rule never to run.'

He put some francs on the table and began walking back to Edith. He went directly to the apartment, making no effort to evade any possible surveillance. If they knew enough to have learned about the Brighton bank account, they would know about his Zürich home.

Edith looked up, smiling, as he entered. The expression faltered when she saw Charlie's face.

'What is it?'

'The Brighton bank has been robbed,' he reported. 'The safe deposit room.'

The fear was immediate. She rose up, without thought, then remained standing in the lounge like a rabbit caught in a poacher's torch, not knowing which way to flee.

'So it's all over,' she said, very softly.

'It could just be coincidence,' he tried, hopefully.

'Don't be damned stupid,' she said. 'You can't believe that.'

She moved at last, going towards the bedroom.

'What are you doing?'

She stopped at the question.

'I'm going to pack, of course.'

'What for, Edith?' he said. He spoke calmly, trying to reduce her apprehension.

She sniggered, control slipping again.

'To get out . . . run . . . what else?'

'We can't run anywhere, Edith.'

She turned fully, to face him.

'What do you mean, we can't go anywhere?'

'Just that.'

'Don't be ridiculous, Charlie.'

'That's exactly what I'm not being. I've got to go back to Brighton, today.'

'Charlie! For God's sake!'

He went forward, taking both her hands in his. Fear was vibrating through her. Poor Edith, he thought, studying her. Poor frightened, abused, trusting, faithful Edith. She'd suffered a great deal because of him, Charlie realised. And never once complained, not even during their most bitter rows. The evidence wasn't overly visible, not physically. Her body was still firm enough to be exciting; the figure of a woman ten years younger, he often assured her. And meant it, quite sincerely. It was in her face that the anxiety had settled, defying the efforts of successive and increasingly

70

more expensive beauticians, lining the pale blue eyes and around her mouth and furrowing the forehead that had once been so smooth and unworried. It would have shown in the greyness of her hair, too, if she hadn't constantly had it disguised during those weekly visits to the beauty salons.

'Edith,' he said, his voice even and deepened by the sadness. 'The one thing we could never sustain is any detailed investigation by a civilian police force . . .'

'But . . .'

'Listen to me, Edith. There's been a robbery estimated at upwards of a million pounds. What would happen if I don't go back, the one box-holder they can't locate? I'll be the prime suspect, the man who rented the facility to obtain access to the deposit room, to plan the robbery.'

'But it's an assumed name,' protested Edith, desperately.

'Which would unquestionably establish the guilt,' he insisted. 'A box-holder who fails to turn up and is then discovered to have taken out the rental under a phoney name . . .'

He paused, waiting for the acceptance to register. Her face remained blank.

' . . . an assumed name,' he resumed. 'That we are currently using on the passports legitimately obtained on forged birth certificates. It would be normal police routine to check for passports, if I don't show up. From the application forms, they would get our pictures . . .'

She went to speak again, but he raised his fingers to her lips, stopping her.

'I know we've got other passports, in your vault here. But the photographs are the one thing we *can't* alter. If I don't return to Brighton, our pictures will be circulated by Interpol distribution within forty-eight hours and there won't be a passport control through which we could pass without identification . . .'

She sagged, like a puppet whose strings had been cut.

'Oh, God,' she said. The lines on her face seemed to deepen.

He led her back to the chair, sitting her down.

'I'm taking no risks, going to the police,' he attempted to reassure her. 'I'm not wanted for anything . . . not by them, anyway . . .'

She shook her head.

'I'm confused, Charlie.'

To a degree, so was he, he thought. How soon would he be able to understand completely what was happening?

'It's quite simple,' he said. 'All I have to do is return to Brighton and answer whatever questions the police will want to ask.'

'But the money . . .'

' . . . will be gone,' he cut in. He hoped, he thought. If it had been left, it would need some explanation.

'So all I have to do is name the insurance policies, admit to a small sum they will expect me to have had lodged there and that'll be the end of it . . .'

The dullness had gone from her face, he saw.

'You're forgetting something, Charlie,' she accused him. 'Or perhaps trying to make me forget something.'

'What?'

'That would be all right if we thought the robbery were a coincidence . . .'

'We can't be sure . . .'

'If we thought it were a coincidence,' she repeated, refusing the interruption. 'And we both know it isn't. We both know that you've been found, Charlie. Not just found, either. They've discovered everything about you, Charlie – everything – we're not discussing the end of anything. We're talking about the beginning.'

'There's no proof of that. Not yet.'

'Do you need proof, for heaven's sake?'

'I certainly need more than we've got so far before I abandon something it's taken us so long to establish.'

She shook her head.

'You're walking right back to them, Charlie . . . right back to where they can do whatever they like.'

She was right, Charlie accepted. And too intelligent to be

persuaded otherwise. And there was not a thing he could do about it. Not a bloody thing. Bastards.

'The problem is, darling,' he said, feeling the first surges of real fear, 'that I've got no choice. At least this way I gain time to fight back.'

'Fight back!'

She spat the words out, face twisted in disgust. She was very frightened, Charlie accepted.

'Stop it, Charlie,' she demanded. 'Stop all this rubbish about fighting back and survival. Do you realise what you're facing this time?'

'Edith,' he said, avoiding the question, 'we both knew, no matter how much we tried to avoid admitting it, that it could happen, one day.'

Her anger died as quickly as it had erupted.

'Oh, Charlie,' she said, 'I'm so frightened.'

'I'll find a way out,' he promised.

It had been a fatuous thing to say, he realised, seeing the look on her face.

Charlie caught the evening flight to London. He travelled with only hand baggage and was one of the first Swissair passengers through passport control. It was 7.15 p.m.

At 7.35, George Wilberforce received a telephone call at his London flat, confirming the arrival for which he had been alerted by the earlier message from Zürich. He began to hum in time with the stereo and then smiled, in recognition. Delius. He'd played that the night he'd first located Charlie Muffin. And now he'd trapped him. He'd enjoy the satisfaction of the following day's meeting with the Americans, he decided.

Onslow Smith was waiting at the Albemarle Street hotel in which they were both staying when Ruttgers returned from Zürich.

'Everything according to plan?' he greeted the ex-Director.

Ruttgers frowned at the assessment.

'No,' he disagreed. 'He's still alive.'

73

THIRTEEN

Charlie had identified the unmarked police car about twenty yards from the house, so he was waiting for the doorbell when it sounded. He paused, briefly, preparing himself and when he opened the door the expectant smile was carefully in place.

'Yes?'

'Police,' identified the taller of the two men. He produced a warrant card, holding it steadily for Charlie to examine it. 'We . . .'

'Of course,' broke off Charlie. 'Come in.'

He stood back for them to enter. They were both smart but unobtrusive men, grey-suited, muted ties, polished black shoes. Hendon, guessed Charlie.

'Why of course?' demanded the first man, unmoving.

Aggressive, too, decided Charlie. But properly so.

'The robbery,' he said. 'What else?'

'Ah,' said the man. Then waited. It was a practised reaction, realised Charlie, leading them into the lounge. So the older man prided himself on his interrogation technique. He had once, remembered Charlie. He'd been damned good. He hoped it hadn't been too long ago; he felt the tingle of apprehension.

The policeman looked at Charlie and Charlie smiled back.

'So you know about the robbery?' queried the man.

'I didn't get your name?' replied Charlie.

The detective frowned, off-balanced by the response. Then he smiled.

'Law,' he said. 'Superintendent Harry Law.'

He stared at Charlie, expectantly. Charlie gazed back.

'Law,' said the man, again.

Still Charlie said nothing.

'Unusual name for a policeman,' offered the detective, at last. 'Law . . . police . . .'

It was a prepared charade, the clumsy joke at his own expense to put an interviewee falsely at ease, decided Charlie.

'Very unusual,' he allowed, hardly intruding the condescension. On the flight to London, he'd rehearsed the inevitable meeting, deciding on the vague impatience of a rich man.

The superintendent detected the attitude. The smile slipped away, irritably.

Law was an almost peculiar figure, thought Charlie. Smooth, shining-pink cheeks, glistening oiled hair, perfectly combed and in place, eyes wetly bright and attentive. A disconcerting man, Charlie labelled him. Because he chose to be. He would have to be careful. It was not going to be as easy as he had imagined. Perhaps nothing was.

'You knew about the robbery?' Law repeated. There was a hardness to his voice now. The man had almost lost his temper, guessed Charlie. Maybe he wasn't as good an interrogator as he thought he was.

'It's the main item in every newspaper,' pointed out Charlie. 'It would be difficult not to know about it.'

'But you didn't bother to contact the bank?' criticised Law.

The reason for the waiting police car and the visit from such a senior officer within thirty minutes, realised Charlie. It would have been sensible to have telephoned from Switzerland. And even more sensible to have picked upon an alternative reaction to the police approach. He'd never be able to play the rich man as long as he had a hole in his ass. It was too late now to change it; it would increase rather than allay suspicion.

'No,' he admitted. It would be as wrong now to hurry an explanation.

'Why?'

The question thrust from the man, the voice even harder.

'Please sit down,' deflected Charlie. He gestured Law and the other man to a couch in the middle of the room.

'I didn't catch your name, either,' he said, to the younger man, aware as he spoke of the anger stiffening the superintendent's body.

'Hardiman, sir,' responded the young policeman. 'Sergeant John Hardiman.'

'Why?' repeated Law.

Charlie turned back to the man. Very soon, Charlie guessed, the superintendent would become openly rude.

'Didn't I contact the bank?'

Law nodded, breathing deeply. The temper was the man's failing, thought Charlie.

'I didn't want to be a nuisance,' explained Charlie simply.

Law frowned.

'Forgive me, sir,' he said. 'I don't follow.'

A clever recovery, assessed Charlie. Seize the apparent conceit of the person you're interviewing and convey the impression they're far more intelligent than you, so they'll over-reach themselves.

'The newspapers talked of the value being in the region of a million pounds,' said Charlie.

'Could be,' agreed Law. 'Once we establish the contents of the deposit boxes.'

'Quite,' said Charlie, as if that were sufficient explanation. 'So I didn't want to be a bother.'

There was another sigh from the older detective.

'You're still not making yourself clear.'

'Can I offer you a drink?' Charlie slipped away again. He gestured towards the drinks tray. Law had begun to perspire, he saw. Charlie decided he wan't doing too badly.

'Whisky would be very nice, sir,' accepted Law. The man fitted a smile into place, the protective mask behind which he was determined to operate.

Charlie went to the bottles and poured Scotch for himself and the superintendent. Hardiman hesitated, then shook his head in refusal.

'You were telling me you didn't want to be a nuisance,' encouraged the superintendent.

'Yes,' said Charlie. 'I imagined that people who had had valuables in their boxes would be inundating the bank with telephone calls and visits and I thought my enquiries could wait until tomorrow.'

Slowly Law placed the glass on a side table that Charlie had positioned close to him and nodded to Hardiman. The younger man took a notebook from his pocket.

'I see,' said Law, slowly. 'So there was nothing valuable in your box?'

'Not valuable in the terms of the robbery,' said Charlie. 'Some insurance policies ... the lease to this house and the conveyancing documents ... that sort of thing.'

'Just papers?' demanded Law.

'And a little money ... perhaps £500 ...'

The superintendent sipped his drink again.

'You don't know the actual amount?'

He let the disbelief leak into the question.

'I travel a great deal,' said Charlie. 'The odd bits of currency and travellers' cheques I don't spend I normally put into the box for use another time. So I can't give you the precise figure, no.'

'But it certainly wouldn't be more than £500?'

'Certainly not,' said Charlie.

He waited, disguising the apprehension. If the money had been left, as Sir Archibald would have decreed it should if he had organised the operation, then this would be the moment when he lost the encounter, Charlie knew. A formal accusation of lying, maybe even the official warning under Judges' Rules and then the request to accompany them to the police station for further questioning.

Law was nodding, disclosing nothing. Hardiman was busily writing in the notebook.

'Isn't that rather expensive?' asked the superintendent, ending the pause.

'Expensive?' asked Charlie. His voice almost broke, showing anxiety. Had the money been there, they would have challenged him immediately, he knew. He felt the first bubble of hope.

'Hiring a safe deposit box for the sort of stuff most people keep in a cupboard drawer?' enlarged the detective.

Charlie forced the smile.

'Ironic, isn't it?' he said. 'I'm the sort of person who likes to know everything is safe . . . so I put it in a bank because I thought there was less chance of a robbery than here, in the house.'

'Ironic,' agreed Law.

But it wasn't agreement, guessed Charlie. There was still doubt.

The superintendent emptied his glass and shook his head in refusal when Charlie gestured towards the bottle.

'You wouldn't mind if I checked with your insurance companies about the policies?'

'Of course not,' said Charlie. 'The Sun Life of Canada and the Royal Assurance.'

Hardiman noted the names.

'Hope I haven't caused difficulties,' said Charlie.

'Difficulties?' queried Law.

'By not bothering to contact the bank . . . you seemed to attach some importance to it.'

'It appeared odd,' allowed Law.

'And I was just trying to be helpful,' repeated Charlie.

'Yes, sir.'

Law paused, then demanded again: 'There was nothing more than the policies, documents concerning this house and the small amount of money?'

'Nothing,' Charlie assured him. The insurance had been Edith's idea, he remembered; being normal, she'd called it.

Both men were staring at him, he realised. A silence settled into the room. Charlie stayed perched on the edge of the armchair, curbing any indication of nervousness.

'Then you're lucky,' said Law, at last.

'Lucky?'

'The policies weren't even taken . . . so you won't have to bother with duplicates.'

Charlie nodded. He'd got away with it, he thought. The realisation swept through him. The two detectives still didn't seem completely satisfied.

'That's very fortunate,' said Charlie.

'Yes,' said Law. 'Very fortunate.'

'The money's gone, I suppose?' asked Charlie.

'Yes,' confirmed the superintendent. 'All five hundred pounds of it.'

Again the policeman waited, letting the sarcasm settle. So it was the smallness of the amount they couldn't accept. Another mistake, like the artificial attitude.

'So I'm lucky all the way around,' said Charlie.

'Sir?' questioned the superintendent.

'That it *was* only £500,' expanded Charlie. 'It's enough, but not as much as the other people seem to have lost.'

'No, sir,' accepted Law. There was still doubt, Charlie gauged.

'You say you travel a great deal, sir?' pressed Law.

'I have a home in Switzerland as well as here,' said Charlie. 'I move between the two very frequently.'

'That must be nice,' said Law.

He managed always to convey the impression that he expected more from any sentence, decided Charlie. It was an interesting technique.

'It is,' he said. 'Very nice.'

'How long do you plan to be here this time, sir?' asked the superintendent.

Charlie delayed answering, guessing some point to the question.

'I don't know,' he shrugged. 'A week ... maybe two ... depends on business.'

'What business?'

The query was abrupt again, cutting across Charlie's generalisation.

Charlie grew cautious again, recognising the danger.

'Investment,' he said. 'Finance ... that sort of thing.'

Both detectives stared, waiting for more.

When he didn't continue, Law prompted: 'You're a financier?'

'My passport describes me as a clerk. But I suppose financier is a better description,' smiled Charlie.

'Any particular firm?'

'Predominantly Willoughby, Price and Rowledge,' responded Charlie easily. 'I deal with Mr Willoughby.'

'A financier,' picked up the superintendent. 'Yet you only kept £500 in a safe deposit box?'

'Exactly,' retorted Charlie. 'Money that isn't working for you is dead ... useless. No one who's interested in making money leaves it lying around in safe deposit boxes.'

'And you are interested in making money, sir?' asked Law, unperturbed.

'Isn't everyone?' asked Charlie.

Law didn't reply immediately, appearing to consider the question.

'And where will you be going, after one or two weeks?' he demanded, changing direction.

'Back to Switzerland,' said Charlie.

'You could let us have an address, of course?'

'Of course,' agreed Charlie. 'But why should you need it?'

The superintendent smiled apologetically.

'Never know, sir. Things come up that you can't anticipate. Always handy to be able to contact people.'

Charlie nodded.

'And I'd like a formal statement,' continued Law. 'Could you come to the station tomorrow?'

Charlie hesitated, a busy man remembering other appointments.

'I suppose so,' he said, at last.

'We'd appreciate that,' said Law.

The approach had changed, realised Charlie.

'Naturally I'll come.'

'You know,' said Law, extending the apparent friendliness. 'Of all the people we've interviewed, you're probably the most fortunate.'

'How's that, superintendent?'

'Apart from the money ... and as you say, that's not a great deal ... you've lost practically nothing.'

'Except my faith in the safety of British banks,' suggested Charlie, trying to lighten the mood.

Law didn't smile.

'In every other box there was more money ... jewellery ... stuff like that. Really you are very lucky,' insisted the superintendent.

'Very lucky,' concurred Charlie.

Law looked hopeful, as if expecting Charlie to say more.

'Is there anything else I can do to help?' asked Charlie. He shouldn't seem too eager to end the meeting, he knew. But equally it would be a mistake to abandon the attitude with which he'd begun the encounter, wrong though he now knew it to be. It was the sort of change Law would recognise.

The superintendent gazed directly at him. Then he shook his head.

'Not at the moment, sir. Just make the statement, tomorrow, if you wouldn't mind.'

'Of course not.'

'And let us know if you're thinking of going anywhere,' the detective continued.

Charlie allowed just the right amount of time to elapse.

'All right,' he said.

'And perhaps tomorrow you could let my sergeant have the Swiss address?'

Charlie nodded.

'Tomorrow, then,' said Law, standing. Immediately Hardiman followed.

'Good night, sir,' said Law.

'Good night, superintendent. Don't hesitate to contact me if I can do anything further to help.'

'Oh we won't, sir,' Law assured him. 'We won't hesitate for a moment.'

Charlie stood at the doorway until he saw them enter their car and then returned to the lounge. He'd just got away with it, he judged, pouring himself a second whisky.

But only just. Not good enough, in fact. He'd lost his edge, in two years. So he'd better find it again, bloody quickly.

'Otherwise, Charlie, your bollocks are going to be on the hook,' he warned himself.

He looked curiously at the whisky, putting the glass down untouched.

'And that's how they got there last time,' he added into the empty room.

For several minutes the policemen sat silently in the car. The lights of Palace Pier were appearing on the left before Law spoke.

'What do you think?' he asked Hardiman.

'Cocky,' replied the sergeant, immediately. He'd been waiting for the question.

'But involved?'

Hardiman shook his head.

'Would you rent a box to discover the layout practically next door to your own house? And having pulled off a million-pound robbery, risk coming back and being questioned, even if you had been that stupid in the first place?'

Law moved his head, in agreement.

'Hardly,' he said. 'They're big points in his favour.'

The car entered the town, pulling away from the sea-front.

'There was something though, wasn't there?' said Hardiman.

Law smiled at the other man's reservations.

'Couldn't lose the feeling that he was used to interrogation . . . didn't have the uncertainty that most people have . . . the natural nervousness that causes them to make silly mistakes,' he confirmed.

'Yet he *was* nervous,' expanded Hardiman.

'Know something else that struck me as odd?' continued Law.

'What?'

'For a financier, he was a scruffy bastard.'

'Yes,' agreed the sergeant. 'Still, don't they say that only the truly rich can afford to dress like tramps?'

'And can you really believe,' went on the superintendent, ignoring the sergeant's remark, 'that a financier with a house like he's got here and who openly admits to another home in Switzerland would only have five hundred quid in a safe deposit box?'

'No,' agreed Hardiman, as the car entered the police station compound. 'But he's not the first one we've encountered on this job who's lied about the amount. That's just tax avoidance, surely?'

'Probably,' said Law. He started to get out of the car, then turned back into the vehicle, towards the other man.

'Let's just keep an eye on him,' he said. 'Don't want to waste any men on full-time observation, but I want some sort of check kept.'

'Good idea,' agreed Hardiman. 'Who knows what we might come up with?'

'Who knows?' echoed the superintendent.

Despite a friendship that stretched back more than two decades, there had been few meetings with Berenkov since his repatriation to Moscow from British imprisonment, General Valery Kalenin accepted. Too few, in fact. He enjoyed the company of the burly, flamboyant Georgian. The K.G.B. chief smiled across the table, offering the bottle.

Berenkov took the wine, topping up his glass.

'French is still best,' he said, professionally. 'More body.'

During his twenty years in London, Berenkov had developed the cover as a wine importer, which had allowed him frequent trips to Europe for contact meetings, into an enormously successful business.

'Not the sort of remark a loyal Russian should make,' said Kalenin, in mock rebuke. 'You'll have to get used to Russian products from now on.'

'That won't be difficult,' said Berenkov, sincerely.

Kalenin pushed aside the remains of the meal he had cooked for them both in his bachelor apartment on Kutuzovsky Prospect. Berenkov had enjoyed the food, the other Russian knew.

'Glad to be back?' Kalenin asked, caught by the tone in the man's voice.

Berenkov nodded.

'I'd had enough,' he admitted. 'My nerve was beginning to go.'

Kalenin nodded. Now Berenkov could lead a pampered life in the Russian capital, he thought, teaching at the spy college to justify the large salary to which he was entitled after the success of such a long operational life, spending the week-ends at the dacha and the vacations in the sunshine of Sochi.

'You did very well,' Kalenin praised him. 'You were one of the best.'

Berenkov smiled at the flattery, sipping his wine.

'But I got caught in the end,' he said. 'There was someone better than me.'

'Law of averages,' said Kalenin. Should he tell Berenkov? he wondered. The man had developed a strong feeling for Charlie Muffin, he knew. A friendship, almost.

'Charlie has been trapped,' he announced bluntly, making the decision.

Berenkov stared down into his wine, his head moving slowly, a man getting confirmation of long-expected bad news.

'How?' he asked.

Kalenin gestured vaguely.

'I don't know,' he said. 'But from the amount of leakage it's obvious the British want it recognised they intend creating an example out of him.'

'Charlie would have expected it, of course,' said Berenkov distantly.

Kalenin said nothing.

The former spymaster looked up at him.

'No chance of your intervening, I suppose? To give him any help?'

Kalenin frowned at the suggestion.

'Of course not,' he said, in genuine surprise. 'Why ever should I?'

'No, of course not,' accepted Berenkov. 'Stupid of me to have mentioned it.'

'He's still alive, apparently,' volunteered Kalenin. 'It's not at all clear what they are going to do.'

'Charlie was very good,' said Berenkov. 'Very good indeed.'

'Yes,' agreed Kalenin. 'He was.'

'Poor Charlie,' said Berenkov.

'More wine?' invited Kalenin.

'Thank you.'

FOURTEEN

Perhaps, thought Wilberforce, arranging the money on the desk for everyone to see had been too theatrical. Onslow Smith was openly smirking, he saw, annoyed. That would stop, soon enough. The time had passed when people laughed at George Wilberforce; and from today they would begin to realise it.

'Just over two hundred thousand dollars,' said the British Director, indicating the money. 'About half of what was stolen from you ... and no affidavits that might have caused problems.'

'So now we kill him,' Ruttgers interrupted impatiently.

'No,' said Wilberforce simply.

For several moments there was no sound from any of the men in the room. It was Sir Henry Cuthbertson who broke the silence.

'What do you mean, no?' he demanded. 'We've achieved what we set out to do. Let's get the whole stupid business over.'

'No,' repeated Wilberforce. 'There are other things tó do first.'

'Director,' said Onslow Smith, trying with obvious difficulty to control himself, 'this affair began with the intention of correcting past problems. We've put ourselves in a position of being able to do so. Let's not risk making any more.'

'I intend teaching the Russians a lesson,' announced Wilberforce.

'You're going to do *what*?'

Onslow Smith's control snapped and he looked at the other Director in horror. The damned man was on an ego trip, he realised.

'For almost two years they've mocked and laughed ... *I've* been ridiculed. Now I'm going to balance the whole thing.'

'Now wait a minute,' said Onslow Smith urgently. He stood up, nervously pacing the room. 'We agreed, not a month ago, that what we were attempting to do was dangerous ...'

He looked intently at the Briton for reaction. Wilberforce nodded.

'But it worked,' continued Smith. 'Charlie Muffin is now back in England. We can do anything we like with him. So now we just complete the operation as planned and invite no more problems.'

'There will be no problems,' insisted Wilberforce, quietly. They were all very scared, he decided.

'With Charlie Muffin, there's always risk,' said Braley breathily, risking the impertinence. Surreptitiously he slipped an asthma pill beneath his tongue.

'How do you intend teaching the Russians a lesson?' asked Cuthbertson.

From the rack on his desk, Wilberforce selected a pipe and began revolving it between his fingers. Sometimes, he thought, he felt like a kindergarten teacher trying to instil elementary common sense. It would be pleasant hearing them apologise for their reluctance in a few days' time.

'I've already seen to it that the Russians know we've located the man,' he admitted.

'Oh, Christ!' blurted Onslow Smith, exasperated. Already, he thought, it might be too late.

Wilberforce shook his head sadly at the reaction.

'And tonight, for a little while at least, we are going to borrow the Fabergé collection that has just arrived from Russia for exhibition here.'

'You're going to do *what*?'

Onslow Smith appeared in a permanent state of shocked surprise.

'Take the Fabergé collection,' repeated Wilberforce.

'The Russians will go mad,' predicted Braley.

'Of course they will,' agreed Wilberforce. 'That is exactly what I intend they should do. And what will they find, when we leak the hint about one of the insurers of the collection? What we found, by elementary surveillance and checking the company accounts after the churchyard encounter with Rupert Willoughby – that their precious Charlie Muffin is a silent partner in the firm.'

'It's lunacy,' said Smith, fighting against the anger. 'Absolute and utter lunacy.'

'No it's not,' insisted Wilberforce. 'It is as guaranteed against fault as the method I devised to get Charlie Muffin back to England.'

'But we can't go around stealing jewellery,' protested Cuthbertson.

'And I'm not interested in settling imagined grievances with Russia. It's over, for Christ's sake. It has been, for years,' said Smith.

'Not with me, it hasn't,' said Wilberforce. He turned to the former Director. 'And I've no intention that we should permanently steal it. The Fabergé collection is priceless, right?'

Cuthbertson nodded, doubtfully.

'But valueless to any thief,' continued Wilberforce. 'He'd never be able to fence it.'

'So why steal it in the first place?' asked Ruttgers.

'For the same reason that such identifiable jewellery is

always stolen,' explained Wilberforce. 'Not to sell or to break up. Merely to negotiate, through intermediaries, its sale back to the insurers who would otherwise be faced with an enormous settlement.'

They still hadn't understood, realised Wilberforce. Perhaps they would, after it had all worked as perfectly as he intended.

'With something as big as this, the insurers are guaranteed to co-operate and buy it back,' he tried to convince them. 'Every piece, apart from those which are absolutely necessary to achieve what I intend, will be back in Leningrad or Moscow within two months. And the only sufferers will be Willoughby's insurance firm who have had to pay up on the missing items. And Charlie Muffin, who will lose the other half of what he stole from you . . . paying America back for something stolen from Russia. Can't you see the irony of it? Charlie Muffin will. That's why I'm letting him stay alive, to see it happen. There's no hurry to kill him now . . . he can't go anywhere and he knows it.'

When there was still no response, Wilberforce pressed on: 'We'll have put the Russians in their place and there won't be a service, either in the West or the East, who won't know about it . . . because I've already made damned sure it's being spelled out, move by move . . .'

'It's very involved,' said Cuthbertson reluctantly.

'And foolproof,' said Wilberforce. 'No risk. No danger.'

'There are too many things over which we haven't any control,' said Ruttgers, through a tobacco cloud. 'Charlie Muffin has only got to do one thing we don't expect and the whole thing is thrown on its ass.'

'But it won't be,' said Wilberforce. 'The jewellery is being taken tonight. Once that goes, everything else follows naturally. It hardly matters what Charlie Muffin does. He's helpless to affect it, in any way. In fact, that's exactly what he is – helpless.'

'What about the civil police?' protested Smith. 'They're already involved in the bank robbery. There's a risk there.'

'We employed a petty crook on that . . . the same one who

will be used tonight. We'll arrange his arrest, so that most of the stuff taken from the Brighton bank can be recovered and returned to its owners – those not too frightened of any tax investigation to claim it, anyway.'

'He'll talk,' said Smith.

'About what?' enquired Wilberforce. 'A mystery man called Brown who seems to have an enormous amount of inside information and knowledge?'

He nodded towards Snare, whose reluctance at the instructions he had been given that night was growing with the objections from the other people in the room.

'The meetings are always arranged by telephone. They've only ever met at crowded railway stations. And they'll part immediately after the Fabergé robbery, just as they separated directly after the Brighton bank robbery. Packer can talk for as long as he likes and it won't matter a damn. He's a villain, with a list of previous convictions. Which is exactly why we chose him. We've even ensured that during the bank robbery he drank from a mug which was left behind, so there will be saliva contrasts for blood type identification. He'll be sufficient for the police, especially when they'll be able to return most of the property. Why can't you accept that there is nothing that can go wrong?'

'Because I'm not convinced it's that easy,' said Smith. He hesitated, then added quietly: 'So I won't agree with it.'

Wilberforce stared back expressionlessly at the other Director. He hadn't expected an outright refusal.

Smith stood up, feeling he had to emphasise his reasons. 'Not only is it dangerous,' he said, 'it's stupid. Because it's unnecessary.'

'I don't really see that there's a great deal you can do to stop it,' pointed out Wilberforce objectively. It was unfortunate he had to be quite so direct, he thought. In many ways, Smith's growing condescension reminded him of his wife. At least, he decided, he'd be able to make Smith express his regret, later on.

For several moments, the two Directors stared at each other and Wilberforce imagined the American was going to argue further. Then Onslow Smith jerked his head towards Ruttgers.

'Let's go,' he said.

As the men walked to the door of the huge office, Wilberforce called out: 'I do hope that you're not severing our co-operation on this matter.'

Smith halted, looking back.

'It was not I who ended the co-operation,' he said.

Neither American spoke until they had settled in the back of the waiting limousine and were heading towards Grosvenor Square.

'We going ahead by ourselves?' asked Ruttgers, expectantly.

'We bring men in,' agreed Smith. 'A lot more than were with you in Zürich.'

'Why?'

Smith didn't answer immediately.

'Wilberforce is a sneaky son of a bitch,' he said, after several minutes' thought. 'I'm not going to get our asses in any snare he's laying for us.'

'I don't understand.'

'Even when you can control the civil police, as Wilberforce can within limitations on a thing like this, a killing is still a killing. I'm not making a move against Charlie Muffin until I'm convinced that Wilberforce isn't setting us up.'

'More delays,' moaned Ruttgers bitterly. 'We're giving the bastard a chance.'

'But we're not making any mistakes,' said Smith. He'd already made too many, imagining there was safety in letting Wilberforce take the lead. It was time, thought Smith, that he started looking after himself. And that was what he was going to do.

Back in the Whitehall office, Cuthbertson stared at the Director's desk he had once occupied.

'They forgot to take the money with them,' he said.

'They'll be back,' said Wilberforce confidently.

Contacting Rupert Willoughby by telephone, instead of

going personally either to his flat or City office, was probably a useless precaution, decided Charlie. But it might just reduce the danger to the younger man. So it was worth while. It was right he should feel guilt at compromising Sir Archibald's son, he knew.

'Warn me?' queried the underwriter.

'The robbery must mean they've found me,' said Charlie. 'It's very easy for the department to gain access to bank account details. If they're aware of the meetings between us, they'll know the £50,000 inheritance has moved from deposit. And probably guessed the other money came from me, as well.'

'Couldn't the robbery just be a coincidence?'

'No.'

'Why not?'

'It's a guaranteed way to get me back here . . . where they can do what they like, when they like and in circumstances over which they'll have most control.'

'Christ,' said Willoughby softly.

Very soon, thought Charlie, the man would appreciate it really wasn't a game.

'I've already had to involve you,' apologised Charlie. 'I've had to make a statement to the police and I gave you as a business reference.'

'They've already contacted me,' confirmed Willoughby. 'I think I satisfied them.'

Law was very thorough, Charlie decided.

'Thank you,' he said.

'I had little choice, did I?' said Willoughby.

The attitude was changing, recognised Charlie.

'What are you going to do?' asked the underwriter.

'I don't understand enough to do anything yet,' said Charlie. He stopped, halted by a thought. If Wilberforce were the planner, he'd get perverse enjoyment moving against the son of the man he considered had impeded his promotion in the department.

'Has anything happened to you in the last few weeks that

you regard as strange?' Charlie continued. 'Any unusual business activity?'

There was a delay at the other end of the line, while the man searched his memory.

'No,' said Willoughby finally.

'Sure?'

'Positive. Whatever could happen?'

'I don't know.'

'You're not very encouraging,' protested Willoughby.

'I'm not trying to be. I'm trying to be objective.'

'What should I do?' asked the underwriter.

'Just be careful,' said Charlie. 'They're bastards.'

'Shouldn't you be the one taking care?'

Charlie grimaced at the question. Wilberforce was using him like a laboratory animal, he thought suddenly, goading and prodding to achieve an anticipated reaction. When laboratory tests were over, the animal was usually killed. When, he wondered, would Wilberforce's experiment end?

'I am,' promised Charlie, emptily.

'When are we going to meet?'

'We're not,' said Charlie definitely.

'Let's keep in touch daily, at least.'

The concern was discernible in the man's voice.

'If I can.'

'My father always said there was one thing particularly unusual about you, Charlie. He said you were an incredible survivor,' recalled Willoughby.

But usually he'd known from which way the attack was coming, thought Charlie. Willoughby had meant the remark as encouragement, he recognised. To which of them? he wondered.

'I still am,' he said.

'I hope so,' said the underwriter.

'So do I,' said Charlie. 'So do I.'

FIFTEEN

Because the northern extension of the Tate Gallery had once been the Queen Alexandra Hospital, occupied by hundreds of people, the sewer complex immediately beneath it was much larger than the other outlets that served the area. They had gone in through a manhole in Islip Street, Snare leading. He was still ahead, guiding the safebreaker, the miner's lamp he wore perfectly illuminating the huge cylindrical passageways.

'What a bloody smell!' protested Johnny. He moved clumsily, feet either side of the central channel, trying to avoid going into the water.

'In Paris, visiting the sewers is considered a tourist attraction,' said Snare. The man was right; it did stink.

'So's eating frogs,' sneered Johnny. Like Snare, he was wearing a hiker's rucksack, bulging with material it had again taken over a week to purchase. In addition, he hauled a collapsible sledge upon which was strapped the drilling motor and heavier equipment. The light from Snare's lamp was sufficient for them both, so Johnny hadn't bothered to turn his on. There was a sudden sound of scurried scratching, and Johnny grabbed out for Snare.

'Rats,' the larger man identified the noise, shrugging the hand away.

Johnny snapped on his light and in his anxiety went in up to his ankle in the water. Snare smiled at the outraged gasp.

'Can't stand rats,' said the safebreaker. He shivered. 'Let's hurry up and get out of here.'

Snare ignored the other man, trying to play his light on to the Department of the Environment plan he'd taken from the sidepocket of his bulging pack. The gallery extension had meant there had been a lot of plans available, he thought gratefully. The sewer route had been marked on the chart in red, with notes on the alarm system and precautions installed overhead.

He heard another splash, an immediate curse and then felt Johnny pressing close to him. Snare pulled away, recalling a medical record he had studied in one of the police files and the assessment why Packer's downfalls invariably involved burly young men of limited intelligence.

'Jesus,' said Johnny, looking over his shoulder. 'Never worked with anyone who managed to get hold of the stuff you do . . . it's like a bloody guide-book.'

'Got a friend,' said Snare. It was the sort of remark the man would remember when he'd been arrested. Might even cause further embarrassment to Willoughby's firm if the man talked about drawings of the sort that insurers might possess.

The tunnel surround began to get smaller and they had to proceed at a crouch.

'Now we're right beneath the original building,' said Snare. Positioning Packer where the narrowing began, Snare carefully measured along the slimy wall, making a mark where he had to begin digging and then insisted on measuring again, to avoid any miscalculation.

He brought another plan from the rucksack, a detailed diagram of all the alarm installations and wiring.

'Where the hell did you get that?' exclaimed Packer.

'Same friend,' said Snare. Confidently he traced their entry hole on to the sewer wall.

'We'll have to work cautiously,' he said, almost to himself. 'There are some vibration alarms in the flooring.'

Snare operated the drill, as he had in Brighton. Again the tool was rubber cushioned, reducing both the noise and the recoil. The man worked very gently, discarding the bits the moment he thought they were becoming blunt and needed a sharper edge to cut into the concrete and brickwork. Frequently he referred to the wiring plan, using a rule to measure the depth of his hole. After about thirty minutes, he put aside the drill, chipping instead with a chisel and rubber-headed hammer, constantly feeling in and scraping away rubble and plaster by hand.

He found the first cluster of wires after an hour. Then he rejected even the hammer, scratching an inch at a time with just the chisel head. When sufficient room had been made, he clamped the carefully prepared bypass leads, with their alligator clips, at either side of the wire cluster and then cut through.

Johnny sighed.

'No sound,' he said.

'There wouldn't have been,' Snare answered. 'This alarm only operates in the Scotland Yard control room.'

Because the adhesive tape they had used for the purpose at Brighton would not have stuck to the slime of the sewer walls, Snare knocked securing hooks into the bricks to hold the bypass leads out of the way.

He used the drill again now, still stopping every few minutes for measurement. It was a further hour before he turned the drill off and began gently prodding at the hole. Suddenly there was a clattering fall of bricks and concrete different from the rest and Snare turned, smiling at the other man.

'The floor,' he said. 'We're through.'

It took thirty minutes before the hole was big enough for them to clamber up, hauling the equipment behind them.

'Thank Christ we're out of there,' said Johnny sincerely. The revulsion shook his body.

Snare motioned him to silence, then checked his watch.

'An hour and forty minutes before there's any guard tour,' he whispered. 'But I don't want any unnecessary sound.'

He'd turned off his miner's headset, using now a large hand-torch with an adjustable cowl, so that the light beam could be accurately controlled. Another plan came from the rucksack.

'The Duneven room is above us and in that direction,' indicated Snare, to his left. 'The photographic room and restaurant is to the right and the stairs up to the ground floor should be immediately behind you.'

Johnny turned, using his own torch, but Snare stopped him.

'Don't forget the bags,' he said.

From the sledge they were leaving near the hole, Johnny took a number of plastic containers, then walked towards the stairway.

At the bottom he paused, awaiting Snare's lead.

'The first six are pressure activated,' said Snare.

He reached past the other man, laying a retractable plank stiffened at either edge by steel rods up to the eighth step.

'Be careful,' he warned.

Hand lightly against the hand-rail for balance, Johnny inched up the ramp. The door at the top was locked and Johnny knelt before it, torch only inches away.

'Piece of cake,' he declared. From his pack he took the dentist's pliers which he had modified since the Brighton robbery, so that the jaws could be locked. Into them he clamped a key blank and impressed it into the lock. Against the impressions he sketched a skeleton and within minutes had shaped a key from steel wire. The lock clicked back on his second attempt.

'Alarm at the top,' cautioned Snare. He pushed past, the magnetised bypass already in his hand. He slipped it over the break and then eased the door open. From his pack he took a wooden wedge, driving it beneath the door edge to prevent it accidentally slamming and disturbing the leads.

Just inside the main hall, Snare went to a panel set into the wall, gesturing for Johnny to follow.

'The first of the two alarm consoles,' he said. 'Open it.'

Johnny used a wire probe this time, easing the tumblers back one by one.

Snare had a plan devoted entirely to the wiring system that suddenly cobwebbed in front of them. He made Johnny hold it, freeing both his hands, and for fifteen minutes worked intently, muttering to himself, fixing jump leads and clamps.

'There,' he said, finally. 'Castrated.'

'You said two?' queried Johnny.

'This is the obvious one,' said Snare. 'The other one is identical but independently wired and concealed.'

It was a floor panel, just inside the cloakroom.

'Clever,' said Johnny, admiringly.

'Unless you know the secrets,' smiled Snare. Practised now, it didn't take him as long to neutralise the second system.

'What now?' asked Johnny.

'Now,' said Snare. 'We just help ourselves if not to the actual crown jewels, as near as makes no difference.'

He paused, checking the time.

'And there's still forty minutes before the attendant patrol.'

The Russian collection was in the main exhibition room, every piece under glass. They stopped, as the torches picked out the jewels of the Fabergé reproductions.

'What's that?' demanded Johnny.

'A miniature jewelled train,' said Snare. 'It's usually kept in the Armoury, in Moscow, along with those Easter egg ornaments in the next case . . .'

'Imagine those in a necklace,' said Johnny, wistfully.

'Beautiful,' agreed Snare. Pity you'd never have a chance to wear it, he thought, cruelly.

'What sort of people have jewelled trains and Easter eggs?' mused Johnny.

'Rich people,' said Snare. 'Very rich people.'

'Didn't they all get killed though?' queried Johnny.

Snare frowned at the qualification.

'Only because they were too stupid to realise the mistakes they were making,' he said.

He moved forward, gesturing to Johnny for the bags he had taken from the sledge. Against the side of each exhibition case he affixed a handle, with adhesive suckers at either tip, then sectioned the glass with a diamond-headed cutter. Gently, to avoid noise, he placed each piece of glass alongside the stand, put each exhibit into a protective chamois leather holder and then, finally, into a bigger container.

Apart from the eggs and the train, Snare took the copies

of the Imperial Crown surmounted by the Balas ruby, the Imperial Orb, topped by its sapphire and the Russian-eagle-headed Imperial Sceptre, complete with its miniature of the Orloff diamond.

Snare lifted the bags, testing their weight.

'Enough,' he decided.

He turned, looking at Johnny.

'You know what you've just done?' he demanded.

'What?'

'Carried out the jewel robbery of the century,' said Snare, simply.

'Now all we've got to do is sell them back,' said Johnny. And then let Herbie Pie and all those other doubting bastards know. But discreetly, so they wouldn't think he was boasting.

'That'll be no trouble,' said Snare, confidently. He was glad there wouldn't be any more burglaries, he decided. From now on he could sit back and watch all the others do the work, enjoy the sport of watching Charlie squirm.

Johnny humped the straps of the bags comfortably on to his shoulders, then followed Snare's lead down the stairs. Neither spoke until they reached the entry hole in the basement floor. Johnny stood, gazing apprehensively into the blackness.

'I'd very happily give back one of those funny eggs to avoid having to go back down there,' he said plaintively.

Snare dropped through first, turning on the beam of his helmet to provide some light. Johnny lowered the jewellery first, then wriggled through, hanging for a moment before letting himself go. He misjudged the drop, stumbling up to his knees in the drainage channel.

'Shit,' he said.

'That's right,' agreed Snare.

They had almost finished the meal in their Moscow apartment when Berenkov apologised, explaining the cause of his silence to Valentina.

'There couldn't be any doubt?' asked the woman.

Berenkov shook his head, positively.

'Comrade General Kalenin was very sure – they've definitely found Charlie.'

She shook her head sadly.

'Poor man.'

'Yes,' he agreed. 'Poor man.'

'Why torture him?'

'I don't know,' he said.

'Just like children . . . cruel children.'

'Yes,' he accepted. 'It's often very childlike.'

'But in the end they'll kill him?'

'Yes,' he said, saddened by the question. 'They will have to do that.'

Valentina didn't speak for several minutes. Then she said, 'Is he married?'

'I think so.'

'It's her I feel sorry for,' said the woman. 'Perhaps more than for him. He knew the risks, after all.'

'Yes,' said Berenkov. 'I suppose he did.'

'I wonder what she'll do?' said Valentina, reflectively.

'You should know, perhaps more than anybody,' Berenkov reminded her impulsively.

His wife looked at him sorrowfully.

'I'd just weep,' she said. She lingered, unsure of the admission.

Then she added: 'Because I wouldn't be brave enough to kill myself.'

SIXTEEN

Onslow Smith had taken over the larger conference chamber in the American embassy in London's Grosvenor Square. He stood on a dais at one end of the room, a projection screen tight against the wall behind him. While he waited for everyone to become seated, he fingered the control button connected to the screening machine that would beam the pictures through the tiny square cut into the far wall.

The diminutive figure of Garson Ruttgers bustled into the room, moving towards the seat which Smith had positioned just off the raised area but still in a spot separating him from the other operatives, a considerate recognition of the importance he had once enjoyed.

Immediately behind sat Braley, clipboard on his knee. It was a great pity, decided the Director, that the Vienna episode had marked the end of any promotional prospects for the man. Braley appeared to have a fine analytical mind and worked without panic, despite the obvious nervous reaction to stress. He'd arranged everything for that day's meeting and done it brilliantly; one of the few people affected by Charlie Muffin who would easily make the transition to a planner's desk.

One of the few people, he repeated to himself, staring out into the room. Eighty men, he counted. Eighty operatives who had been trained to Grade 1 effectiveness; men from whom the Agency could have expected ten, maybe fifteen years of top-class service. All wiped out by Charlie Muffin. And Wilberforce expected him to sit back and do damn all except be the cheerleader. The apparent success of the early part of the entrapment had gone to the British Director's head, he decided.

'Shall we begin?'

The room quietened at the invitation. Smith stood with his hand against the back of the chair, looking down at them.

'Some of you,' he said, 'may have guessed already the point of drafting you all to London . . .'

He waited, unsure at the harshness of the next part of the prepared text. It was necessary, he decided. It would remind them of what they had lost and bring to the surface the proper feelings about the man responsible.

' . . . because you all, unfortunately, shared in the operation that ended your active field careers.'

Ruttgers, who had been initially grateful for the seating arrangement, moved uncomfortably in front of the men he had personally led to disaster, realising too late its drawbacks. Needing the activity, he lighted the predictable cigarette.

'Because of this man . . .' announced Smith, dramatically. He pressed the control button. A greatly enlarged picture, several times bigger than life, of Charlie Muffin appeared on the screen. It had been taken in the churchyard. Several times Smith pressed the button, throwing a kaleidoscope of photographs on the wall, shots of Charlie Muffin in Zürich, coming through passport control at London airport, outside his Brighton house and entering and leaving the offices of Rupert Willoughby.

'Taken,' said Smith, 'by the British.'

He paused to let the murmur which went through the room settle into silence. It was like baiting animals, bringing them to the point where their only desire was to fight, thought the Director.

'Charlie Muffin has been found,' he declared.

He waited again for the announcement to be assimilated.

'Found,' he picked up, 'by a very painstaking but rewarding operation conducted by the British . . .'

There was complete silence in the room, realised Smith. The concentration upon what he was saying was absolute. He sighed, shuffling the prepared speech in his hand.

'I wish to make it quite clear at the outset that since the discovery of the man, the handling of the affair had been jointly handled by the British and ourselves.'

He appeared to lose a sheet of notes, then stared up at them.

'At very high level,' he emphasised.

He waited for them to assess the importance, then went on: 'A certain course had been decided upon, a course of which you've no need to be aware . . .'

Harsh again, recognised Smith. But necessary, a reminder of just how far down they'd all been relegated. After this they'd be clerks at Langley until retirement, with only the Virginia countryside to relieve the boredom.

'It is sufficient for you to know that no immediate action – open action, anyway – is being taken against Charlie Muffin...'

The noise started again, the sound of surprise this time.

'Which does, of course,' continued the C.I.A. chief, 'create a danger.'

He stopped once more. He'd really fucked it up, he decided honestly.

The response from the room was growing louder and several men were trying to catch his attention, to ask questions.

'And that is why I have gathered you here,' said Smith quickly, trying to subdue the clamour. 'The British consider the surveillance they have established is sufficient and certainly, thus far, it has proven to be. But I have no intention whatsoever of this Agency taking a subservient role in the continuing operation envisaged by the British.'

Smith sipped from a glass of water and in the gap a man at the front blurted: 'You mean we are going to stop working with the British?'

Smith smiled, the timing of the question over-riding any annoyance at the interruption.

'I intend giving the impression of continued co-operation,' he said. 'Before this meeting is over, you will all be given dossiers containing every item of information about Charlie Muffin that the British have so far been able to assemble ... it is quite extensive. With the benefit of that information, we are going to establish our own, independent operation. When the shit hits the fan, I still want us wearing clean white suits.'

The persistent questioner in the front row pulled forward· again.

'He will be eliminated, sir, won't he? Charlie Muffin will be eliminated?'

It was almost a plea, thought Smith. He moved to speak,

but Ruttgers responded ahead of him, emotion momentarily washing away his awareness of his reduced role.

'Oh, yes,' said the ex-Director, fervently. 'He'll be eliminated. I promise you that.'

'But not until I've given the explicit order,' instructed Smith.

Charlie stood at the lounge window of the Brighton house, gazing out at the tree-lined avenue. The uniformed policeman who had passed twice was standing at the corner now, stamping his feet against the early evening chill. Where, wondered Charlie, were the others?

He turned into the room, staring at the bottles grouped on the table by the far wall. No, he decided easily. He didn't need it. Not any more.

'What I need,' he told himself, 'is for them to over-reach themselves. Just once.'

And Edith, he thought. He wanted her by him very much. But not yet. He had to get a clearer indication of what was happening before putting her to any more risk than she already faced. Poor Edith.

SEVENTEEN

Charlie arrived in Rupert Willoughby's office an hour after making the telephone call for the confirmation he scarcely needed. The underwriter greeted him with an attitude that swung between nervousness and anger. At last, thought Charlie. He hoped the growing awareness wouldn't affect the man's memory of his father.

'You knew we'd covered the exhibition?' challenged Willoughby immediately. Anger first, Charlie accepted.

'It was obvious,' said Charlie. 'Once I heard of the robbery. And more particularly, what was stolen and from whom.'

'What does it mean?'

'That the department has known from the very beginning of our meeting. That they know I've put money into your firm. That they had you under permanent observation for as long as they've been watching me. And that in one operation they intend hitting back at everyone.'

Willoughby nodded, as if agreeing some private thought. His throat was moving, jerkily.

'No wonder my father was so frightened in the last year,' he said.

'I warned you,' Charlie reminded him.

Willoughby looked at him, but said nothing.

'Tell me about the cover,' said Charlie.

Willoughby pulled a file towards him, running his hand through the papers.

'Completely ordinary,' he said. 'For an exhibition of this value, the government always goes on to the London market, through Lloyd's. For us, it's usually a copper-bottomed profit. Security is absolute but because of the value and alleged risk, we can impose a high premium.'

'How much cover did you offer?'

'Two and a half million,' said Willoughby.

'What happens now?'

'Claim to be filed. And then the squabbling begins, to gain time.'

'You expect a sell back?'

Willoughby looked surprised.

'Of course,' he said. 'That's what always happens in a case like this.'

'What percentage?'

'Varies. Usually ten.'

Charlie laughed, appearing genuinely amused.

'Two hundred and fifty thousand,' he said. 'Exactly what I put in. They don't mean me to misunderstand for a moment, do they?'

'Is it significant?' asked Willoughby.

'Very,' said Charlie. To continue would mean admitting he was a thief. The man deserved the honesty, he decided.

'They want to recover $500,000 from me. Plus interest,' he said. 'They got almost half from the Brighton robbery. This would be the remainder.'

Willoughby sat, waiting. It was impossible to judge from the expression on his face whether there was any criticism.

'You told me once you hadn't done anything criminal,' he accused Charlie.

The anger was on the ascendancy, Charlie decided.

'They set out, quite deliberately, to kill me,' said Charlie. 'That was the penalty I imposed upon them for being abandoned . . . abandoned like your father was. He tried to fight back against them as well, remember. We just chose different ways of doing it. Mine worked better than his. They lost more than money.'

'What happens next?' asked the underwriter.

'I don't know,' confessed Charlie. 'I'd guess they're getting ready to kill me now.'

'You're not worried enough,' said the younger man in sudden awareness. 'Boxed in like this, you should be terrified. Like I am.'

'I'm not,' confirmed Charlie easily. 'The Russian robbery was the error . . . the one I was waiting for them to make . . .'

Willoughby shook his head.

'Your father was very good at this sort of thing,' said Charlie. 'He'd do it to get someone whom he suspected to disclose themselves completely.'

'You're not making yourself clear,' complained the underwriter.

'I *know* the pattern,' said Charlie. 'It must be either Wilberforce or Cuthbertson or both. And I learned from your father a bloody sight better than they did.'

Willoughby gazed back, unconvinced. It was the first time the confidence, almost bordering on conceit, had been obvious, he realised. Another thought came, with frightening clarity. He'd been a fool to become involved, no matter what his feelings for the men who had destroyed his father.

'You've got to get out,' he said.

'Oh, no,' answered Charlie. 'You don't survive looking

constantly over your shoulder. I've tried for the past two years and it's almost driven me mad.'

'You don't have an alternative.'

'I have,' said Charlie. He considered what he needed to say but still began badly, speaking as the thoughts came to him.

'I told you at our first meeting there was a risk of your being compromised,' he said. 'And you have been . . .'

'And I said then that I was prepared to accept that,' interrupted the underwriter in a vain attempt at bravery.

'Because you didn't really know what it was going to be like,' argued Charlie. 'Now it's different. The robbery was directed against you and your firm. And because of it, other underwriters could be out of pocket, coming to a buy-back settlement. From this firm all that is at risk at the moment is the money I've deposited. So this time you've been let off with a warning . . .'

'What do you want?' Willoughby interrupted.

'The sort of help which, if it goes wrong, could mean that next time there won't be any warning,' said Charlie bluntly.

'I'll hear you out,' said Willoughby guardedly.

Charlie stood and began pacing the office, talking as he moved.

'The misjudgment they've made is one that your father never allowed,' lectured Charlie. 'They've given me the opportunity to react.'

'I still don't think you've got any choice,' said Willoughby.

'That's it,' agreed Charlie. 'And that is what Wilberforce and whoever else is working with him will be thinking.'

Charlie stopped walking, thoughts moving sideways.

'Buying back the proceeds of unusual or large robberies isn't particularly uncommon, is it?' he asked suddenly.

'Not really,' said Willoughby. 'Although obviously we don't make a point of announcing it. There's usually some token police objection, as well. Although for political reasons, I don't think that will be very strong in this case.'

'So there are people in this office who wouldn't regard it

as odd if they were asked to behave in a somewhat bizarre way?' Charlie hurried on. 'They'd accept it could be part of some such arrangement?'

'I don't think we've the right to put other people to the sort of danger you seem to think exists.'

'It's not dangerous – not this part,' Charlie assured him. 'I just want them as decoys.'

'I have your promise on that?'

'Absolutely,' said Charlie.

'Then yes,' agreed Willoughby. 'There are people who wouldn't think it at all strange. They might even enjoy it.'

'And what about you?'

'I'm not enjoying any of it any more,' admitted Willoughby, with his customary honesty.

'Well?' asked Charlie nervously.

The underwriter considered the invitation to withdraw.

'Are you going to ask me to do anything illegal? Or involve the firm in any illegality?' he asked, repeating his paramount concern.

'Definitely not.'

'I must have your solemn undertaking.'

'You have it.'

'Then I'll help,' said Willoughby. Quickly, he added: 'With a great deal of reluctance.'

With the number of friends he had, decided Charlie, he could hold a party in a telephone box. And still have room for the band.

'Excellent,' he said enthusiastically. 'Now I think we should celebrate.'

'Celebrate?' questioned Willoughby, bewildered.

'As publicly as possible.'

'I wish I knew what was going on,' protested the underwriter.

'It's called survival,' said Charlie, cheerfully.

It was a tense, hostile encounter, different – although for opposing reasons – from what either the Americans or Wilberforce had anticipated when Smith and Ruttgers had stormed from the office less than twenty-four hours before.

'Well?' insisted Smith.

'It isn't what I expected,' conceded Wilberforce, reluctantly.

'Isn't what you expected!' echoed Smith, etching the disgust into his voice. 'At this moment, Charlie Muffin should be trying to disappear into the woodwork!'

He stood up, moving to a sidetable where copies of the photographs had been laid out. He picked them up, one by one, as he spoke.

'Instead of which,' he said, displaying them to everyone in the room, 'he's practically advertising his presence from the rooftops, drinking champagne at the Savoy until he can hardly stand and then occupying the centre table at the river-view restaurant for a lunch that took almost three hours!'

'He's very clever,' said Cuthbertson, in his wet, sticky voice. 'We shouldn't forget he's very clever.'

'We *shouldn't* forget anything,' agreed Smith. 'Any more than we should have forgotten the point of this operation.'

'It's not been forgotten,' said Wilberforce stiffly.

'Just endangered,' hit back the American Director. 'God knows how badly.'

The Russian robbery had been in England, he thought suddenly. At the moment there was nothing to prove any American involvement. That was how it was going to stay.

'We can't eliminate him, not now,' said Cuthbertson. 'Not until we discover the reason for his extraordinary behaviour.'

'Of course we can't kill him,' accepted Smith, careless of his irritation.

'What do you think it means?' demanded Wilberforce, of Braley.

Braley considered the question with his customary discomfort.

'That there's something we don't know about . . . despite all the checks and investigations, there's obviously something we overlooked ... something that makes Charlie confident enough to act as he's doing.'

Braley blinked at his superiors, worried at the open criticism.

'I've always warned of that possibility,' Wilberforce tried to recover. 'That was the point of the bank entry in the first place, don't forget.'

Smith looked at the other Director in open contempt.

'It could just be a bluff,' said Snare.

'It could be anything,' said Smith. 'That's the whole damned trouble. We just don't know.'

'The Russians are upset,' said Cuthbertson, mildly. The first time anything had gone wrong and Wilberforce was unsettled, he saw. Practically gouging the pipe in half. He smiled, uncaring that the other man detected the expression. Always had thought he could do the job better than anybody else.

'What's happened?' asked Smith.

Wilberforce looked sourly at his one-time chief before replying.

'Formal note of protest to our ambassador in Moscow,' he reported. 'The Russian ambassador here calling at his own request upon the Foreign Secretary and two questions tabled in the House of Commons by some publicity-conscious M.P.s.'

'Hardly more than you expected,' retorted Smith. No one seemed to realise how serious it was, he thought.

'We decided upon a course of action,' said Wilberforce, pushing the calmness into his voice. 'So far every single thing has proceeded exactly as it was planned. Certainly what the man did today was surprising. But that's all it is, a surprise. We mustn't risk everything by attempting ill-considered improvisations.'

'You know, of course,' said Smith, 'that after that lunch he booked into the Savoy?'

'Yes,' said Wilberforce, the irritation returning.

'Another assumed name?' asked Cuthbertson.

Damn the man, thought Wilberforce. The former Director knew the answer as well as any of them.

'No,' he admitted. 'He seemed to take great care to register as Charles Muffin.'

EIGHTEEN

Charlie knew he had registered at the hotel at exactly 3.45 in the afternoon. That concluding act of a flamboyant performance, using his real name, would have confused them sufficiently for at least a two-hour discussion, he estimated. Early evening then. And it would have taken more than twenty-four hours from the moment of decision, even if it had been made in the daytime when people were available, for the necessary warrants and authorisations and then the installation of engineers to put any listening device on the telephone in his hotel room.

Even so, he still went immediately after breakfast to the Savoy foyer to book the call to his Zürich apartment from the small exchange by the lounge stairs, then insisted on taking it in one of the booths from which he could watch the operator.

The first conversation with Edith was abrupt, lasting little more than a minute. Charlie allowed her half an hour to reach the Zürich telephone exchange. She was waiting by one of the incoming booths when he made the second call.

'So you think the apartment here will be monitored?' she said immediately.

'Probably.'

'The robbery wasn't a coincidence, then?'

He smiled to himself at her insistence on an admission. She never liked losing arguments.

'No,' he said. 'Of course not. I was trying to stop you becoming too frightened.'

'You really thought that possible?'

He could detect how strident her voice was. He didn't answer, refusing to argue.

'What else happened?' she demanded.

Briefly, Charlie outlined the details of the Russian robbery and the effect any settlement would have upon Willoughby's firm.

'They know everything about you, Charlie. Everything. You're going to get killed.'

The assertion blurted from her and he heard her voice catch at the other end.

'Edith,' he said patiently, 'I know a way out.'

'There isn't a way out, Charlie,' she said. 'Stop being such a bloody fool.'

He sighed, fighting against the irritation in his voice.

'Did you call to say goodbye, just like you said goodbye to Sir Archibald before you left for Vienna to begin this fucking mess?' she said desperately.

She'd been too long alone, Charlie realised. Now all the fears and doubts were firmly embedded in her mind and refusing to leave. And Edith shouldn't swear, he thought. She paraded the words artificially, like a child trying to shock a new schoolteacher.

'I called to say I loved you,' said Charlie.

The tirade stopped, with the abruptness of a slammed door.

'Oh, Christ, Charlie,' she moaned.

He winced at the pain in her voice. She would be crying, he knew.

'I mean it,' he said.

'I know you do.'

'I love you and I'm going to get us out of all this. We'll find another place...'

'... to hide?' she accused him.

'Has it been that bad?'

'It's been terrible, Charlie. And you know it. And you'd never be able to make it any different, even if you got away from it now.'

He had no argument to put against that, Charlie realised.

'You should have told me how you felt . . . before now,' he said.

'What good would it have done?'

None, he accepted. She was right. As she had been about the drinking and the damned cemetery and everything else.

'I'm sorry, Edith,' he said.

'So am I, Charlie,' she said, unhelpfully.

'I need your help,' said Charlie. At least, he thought, she'd have something more than fear to occupy her mind.

'Of course,' she said. Depression flattened her voice.

'We'll need the other passports,' he said. 'Now that they know our identity the ones we've got aren't any good, not any more.'

He heard her laugh, an empty sound.

'For when you've beaten them all, Charlie?' she asked sadly.

'We're going to try, for God's sake,' he said. The shout would carry beyond the box, but he knew he had to break through the lassitude of defeat.

'Yes,' she agreed, trying to force a briskness into her voice. 'At least we must try.'

The effort failed; she was convinced of failure, he realised.

'Do you have a pen and paper?'

'Of course.'

'I want you to draw the passports from your bank and then travel, by ferry, to England.'

He paused.

'Yes?' she prompted. The dullness was still evident.

'Hire a car,' he continued. 'Then set out at your own pace, touring around the countryside.'

'Charlie . . . ?' she began, but he stopped her.

'Wait,' he said. 'But I want you every third night to be at these hotels . . .'

Patiently he recited from an A.A. guide book the first listing and then the hotel once removed in case the initial choice was full in towns selected from a carefully calculated, sixty-mile radius of London. It took a long time because Charlie insisted she read them back to him, to ensure there was no mistake.

'Start from Oxford,' he concluded, 'the day after to-morrow and go in order of the towns as I've given them to you.'

'And just wait until you contact me at any one of the hotels, always on the third day?' she anticipated.

'That's right.'

'Sounds very simple,' she said and he started to smile, hoping at last for a change in her attitude.

'There's just one thing, Charlie,' she added.

'Yes?'

'What happens after a month, when I've gone around and around and you haven't contacted me . . . haven't contacted me because you're lying dead in some ditch somewhere?'

Her voice switchbacked and she struggled to a halt.

'I don't expect to be lying dead somewhere,' he said.

'But what if you *are*?' she insisted. 'I've got to know, for Christ's sake!'

Very soon she would be crying, he knew. He hoped she was in one of the end boxes at the Zürich exchange where there would be some concealment from the high wall.

'Then it will be Rupert who calls you,' he admitted, reluctantly.

For several minutes there was complete silence.

'It would mean we'd never see each other again, Charlie.'

She was fighting against the emotion, he realised, care-fully choosing the words before she spoke.

'Yes,' he said.

'Funny, isn't it,' she went on, straining to keep her voice even. 'That never really registered with me, the day you left to go to London. But that could be it; the last time. And you didn't kiss me, when you left.'

'I said I don't expect to be lying dead somewhere,' he repeated, desperately.

'What would I do, Charlie?' she pleaded. 'I've always had you.'

Now it was his voice that was flat, without expression. It wouldn't be the answer she wanted, he knew.

'You haven't done anything wrong,' he said. 'Not to them, I mean. So they wouldn't try to hurt you.'

'So I could come safely back here, to an apartment where you'd never be again and to a bed in which you'd never sleep or touch me and . . .'

Grief washed over the bitterness.

' . . . and live happily ever after,' she finished badly, through the sobs.

'Please, Edith,' he said.

He waited, wincing at her attempts to recover.

'I'm sorry,' she said, finally. 'I can't help blaming you and I know all the time that it's not your fault . . . not in the beginning, anyway.'

'We can still win,' he insisted.

'You really believe that, don't you?' she challenged. 'You can't lose that bloody conceit, no matter what happens to you.'

If I did, thought Charlie, then I'd be slumped weeping in a telephone box.

'I mean it,' he tried again, avoiding another confrontation.

'I'll be at Oxford,' she sighed, resigned to the plan.

'I love you, Edith,' he said again.

'Charlie.'

'What?'

'If . . . if you're right . . . if you manage it . . . promise me something.'

'What?'

'You'll tell me that more often.'

'Every day,' he said, too eagerly.

'Not every day,' she qualified. 'Just more than you have in the past.'

The telephone operator looked up at him, eyebrows raised, when Charlie left the box. It had been very hot in the tiny cubicle, he realised. His shirt was wet against his back.

'Thirty-five minutes,' said the man. 'It would have been far more comfortable in your room.'

'Probably,' agreed Charlie.

Edith wouldn't have left the booth in Zürich yet, he knew. She'd be crying.

The pipe stem snapped, a sudden cracking sound in the silent room.

'Sure?' asked Cuthbertson.

'Positive,' said Wilberforce.

'Why would the Americans impose their own surveillance?'

'Because they don't trust ours. Probably don't trust us, either. No reason why they should.'

'They won't kill him?' demanded Cuthbertson, worriedly.

'No,' Wilberforce assured him. 'Not until they've found out why he's doing these things.'

'So what are we going to do?'

'Nothing,' said the British Director. 'It might be a useful safeguard.'

The man was bewildered by Charlie Muffin's attitude, Cuthbertson knew. Served him right; always had been too conceited by half. He coughed, clearing the permanently congested throat.

'Not going quite as we expected,' suggested Cuthbertson.

'No,' admitted Wilberforce.

Upon whom, wondered Cuthbertson, would the man try to put the responsibility this time?

NINETEEN

The lunch with Willoughby was as open as that of the previous day, but kept to a much tighter schedule. For that reason they ate at the Ritz, because the bank Charlie had carefully chosen was a private one less than five hundred yards away in Mayfair and he wanted to begin on foot.

They left at three o'clock. Charlie paused outside, handing Willoughby the document case while he struggled into a Burberry, turning the collar up under the dark brown trilby hat.

'You look rather odd,' said Willoughby.

'Glad to hear it,' said Charlie. 'Let's hope others think so too.'

'I'd hate to think we're wasting our time,' said the underwriter.

'We're not,' Charlie assured him. 'Believe me, we're not.' I hope, he thought.

He led the way through the traffic stop-starting along Piccadilly and up Stratton Street.

An assistant manager was waiting for the appointment that Charlie had made by telephone, one of several calls he had made after speaking to Edith. The formalities were very brief, but Charlie lingered all alone in the safe deposit vault, keeping strictly to the timing that had been rehearsed with the others in Willoughby's office. Edith would have already decided her route and timetable, thought Charlie, sighing. Maybe even packed. She always liked doing things well in advance.

He and Willoughby left the bank at three-fifty, turning up Curzon Street towards Park Lane.

'We're running to the minute,' said Charlie.

'Are you *sure* we're being followed?' asked Willoughby.

'Stake my life on it,' said Charlie, smiling at the unintended irony. 'In fact, I am,' he added.

'I feel rather ridiculous,' said Willoughby.

'You're supposed to feel scared,' said Charlie.

Four o'clock was striking as they emerged in front of the park. For several seconds they remained on the pavement, looking either way, as if seeking a taxi.

'Here we go,' said Charlie, seeing a break in the traffic stream and hurrying across towards the underground car park. The limousine came up the ramp as they reached the exit and the chauffeur hardly braked as Charlie and Willoughby entered. It slotted easily into the stream of vehicles, heading north towards Marble Arch.

'Now I feel scared,' confessed Willoughby.

'There's nothing illegal,' Charlie said.

The halt outside the Marble Arch underground station was purposely sudden, causing a protest of brakes from the line of cars behind, but before the first horn blast Charlie and Willoughby were descending the stairs. They caught the train immediately, an unexpected advantage. As he sat down, Charlie looked at his watch. They were two minutes ahead of schedule, he saw.

'Only another ten minutes and we'll see the beginning of the rush hour,' he said.

Willoughby nodded, without replying. He was staring straight ahead, tight-lipped. The man *was* scared, Charlie realised.

They jerked away from the train at Oxford Circus almost as the doors were closing, going up the escalator on the left and walking swiftly. The car pulled smoothly into the kerb as they emerged, turned quickly left through the one-way system into Soho and then regained Regent Street.

'I wish we could go faster,' muttered Willoughby.

'Speed isn't important,' said Charlie.

There was no need for the braking manoeuvre at Piccadilly station because there was a traffic jam. Charlie led again, bustling down the stairs. This time they sat without speaking until they reached Green Park. As they came up beneath the shadow of the hotel in which they'd eaten, one of Willoughby's clerks, wearing a Burberry, trilby and carrying a document case fell into step with them and the three of them entered the vehicle.

'There's still a car with us,' volunteered the driver, taking a traffic light at amber and accelerating into the underpass on the way to Knightsbridge.

They got out at Knightsbridge station and as they descended the stairway a second clerk, dressed identically to the first and also carrying a matching case, joined the group. They travelled only as far as South Kensington, but when they emerged for the car this time, one of the raincoated men turned away, walking quickly into Gloucester Road. There was another clerk at Victoria and this time they went on for two stations, getting off at the height of the rush hour at Embankment. The throng of people covered the delay of the car reaching them. They travelled north again, to Leicester Square, and when they got out this time, the man who had left them in Kensington was waiting, joining without any greeting until Holborn. They crowded into the car, sped down Southampton Row and then boarded a District Line train at Temple. The car turned, going back along the Strand, circling Trafalgar Square, then pulled in for petrol in St Martin's Lane.

On the underground, the group changed at Monument station, caught a Northern line train and disembarked unhurriedly at Bank. According to the prearranged plan, they waited outside the underwriter's office for the car. It took five minutes to arrive.

'Let's go inside, shall we?' said Willoughby, to the three clerks.

'So where's the Fabergé collection?' quietly complained one of the three men. 'Lot of stupid bloody rubbish.'

He'd missed the 6.30 to Sevenoaks and now his wife would be late for her pottery classes.

'You got a new raincoat out of it,' reminded the man next to him.

'Bought one last week,' said the clerk. 'Sod it.'

To the others in the room, it seemed like blind, irrational rage, but Wilberforce's emotion was really fear, matched almost equally with self-pity. Now the Director sat hunched forward at his desk, even the pipes temporarily forgotten.

'How could it have happened?' he demanded, wearily. 'How the hell could it have possibly happened?'

A sob jerked his voice and he coughed quickly, to disguise it from the others in the room.

'We never considered he would be able to get that much help,' said Snare. 'We just couldn't adjust quickly enough.'

'It was a brilliant manoeuvre,' added Cuthbertson.

'We should do something to Willoughby,' said Snare vehemently.

'What?' demanded Wilberforce. 'There's no law against playing silly buggers on an underground train. And we've already ensured his firm is going to lose money.'

'Frighten him, at least,' maintained Snare.

'Aren't there more important things to worry about?' asked Cuthbertson.

'Christ,' moaned Wilberforce, in another surge of self-pity. 'Oh, Christ.'

A secretary tried to announce the arrival of the Americans, but Smith and Ruttgers followed her almost immediately into the room. Braley's entry was more apologetic.

'Lost him!' challenged the American Director. It was a prepared accusation, the outrage too false.

'And what happened to your men?' retorted Wilberforce instantly.

Smith hesitated, disconcerted that his separate operation had been discovered.

'Just a precaution,' he tried to recover.

'Which didn't work. So it was a stupid waste of time and effort,' said Wilberforce, refusing to be intimidated. 'We've both made a mess of it and squabbling among ourselves isn't going to help. Recovery is all that matters now.'

'How, for God's sake?' asked Smith. 'By now Charlie Muffin could be a million miles away.'

'I had men at every port and airport within an hour,' said Wilberforce, anxious to disclose some degree of expertise. 'He's still here, somewhere.'

'But just where, exactly?' asked Cuthbertson. The other man hadn't offered any sympathy after the Vienna débâcle, remembered the ex-soldier. At one enquiry he'd even sat openly smiling.

Wilberforce shook his head, impatient with the older man's enjoyment of what was happening.

'He's shown us how,' said Wilberforce, quietly. They could still recover, he determined. Recover and win.

'You surely don't mean ...' Snare began to protest, but the Director spoke over him.

'He went into the bank with a document case,' said Wilberforce. 'And we know he opened a safe deposit because we've already checked.'

'No,' tried Snare again, anticipating his superior's thoughts.

'We haven't got anything else,' said the British Director.

'We've carried out two robberies!' protested Snare, looking to the others in the room for support. 'We can't risk another one. It's ludicrous. We're practically turning ourselves into a crime factory.'

'What risk?' argued Wilberforce. 'You've gone in knowing the details of every alarm system and with every architect's drawing. There's never been any danger.'

'We're breaking the law ... over and over again.'

'For a justifiable reason,' said Wilberforce, disconcerted by the strength of the other man's argument.

'I think it's unnecessarily dangerous,' said Snare, aware he had no support in the room. 'What Charlie did was nothing more than an exercise to lose us ... a trick to get us interested, like staying overnight in the Savoy – nothing more than that.'

'But we've got to *know*,' insisted Wilberforce.

'Why can't somebody else do it?' asked Snare, truculently, looking at the Americans. He'd taken *all* the chances, he realised. It was somebody else's turn.

'How can it be someone else?' replied Smith, impatiently. 'You're the only one who can operate with Packer.'

'Too dangerous,' repeated Snare, defeated.

'It's not the only lead,' Ruttgers said quietly.

Everyone turned to him, waiting.

'You've forgotten the wife,' continued the former Director. 'Eventually he'll establish contact with her ... she's the key.'

Both Directors nodded. Cuthbertson shuffled through

some papers, finally holding up that morning's report from the Savoy Hotel.

'There was a thirty-five minute telephone call to Zürich,' he said.

'To a number on the main exchange ... a number upon which we could not have installed any device,' enlarged Ruttgers.

Wilberforce's smile broadened and he reached out for an unfortunate pipe.

'It's getting better,' he said.

'I'll go,' said Ruttgers, quickly. 'I went before ... know the apartment and the woman.'

He looked up, alert for any opposition.

'All right,' agreed Wilberforce immediately. He couldn't remain in complete control any longer, he decided. Didn't want to, either. Finding Charlie Muffin again was the only consideration now. That and spreading some of the blame if anything went wrong.

'Yes,' accepted Smith, doubtfully. It was going to be a difficult tightrope, he thought. So it was right that someone of Ruttger's seniority should be in charge.

The American Director looked back to Snare.

'It's still vital to find out what's in that bank,' he said. 'Even though the idea of a third entry offends me as much as it does you.'

'I've already got men obtaining detailed drawings of the houses on either side from the architects involved and all the protection systems from the insurance companies,' said Wilberforce.

So it had been a pointless objection anyway, Snare realised. They were bastards, all of them.

'Could we be ready tomorrow night?' asked Smith.

'It would mean hurrying,' said Wilberforce.

The American looked at him, letting the criticism register.

'Isn't that exactly what it *does* mean?' he said.

When it became completely dark in the office garage,

Charlie eased himself up gratefully from the floor, stretching out more comfortably on the back seat of the car. He cat-napped for three hours, aware he would need the rest later, then finally got out, easing the cramp from his shoulders and legs. His chest hurt from being wedged so long over the transmission tunnel, he realised. And his new raincoat had become very creased. It seemed more comfortable that way.

Using the key that Willoughby had given him that morn-ing, he let himself cautiously out of the garage side door, standing for a long time in the deep shadows, seeking any movement. The city slept its midnight sleep.

He walked quickly through the side-streets, always keep-ing near the buildings, where the concealment was better. He'd used the cover like this in the Friedrichstrasse and Leipzigerstrasse all those years ago, he remembered, when they'd tried to kill him before. They'd failed that time, too.

The mini, with its smoked windows, was parked where Willoughby had guaranteed the chauffeur would leave it.

The heater was operating by the time Charlie drove up the Strand. Gradually he ceased shivering. It was 12.15 when Charlie positioned the car in the alley which made the private bank so attractive to his purpose, aware before he checked that it would be completely invisible to anyone in the main thoroughfare.

Quietly he re-entered the vehicle, glad of its warmth. It probably wouldn't be tonight, he accepted. But the watch was necessary. Would they be stupid? he wondered.

'If they are, then it'll be your game, Charlie,' he said, quietly. 'So be careful you don't fuck it up, like you have everything else so far.'

TWENTY

Superintendent Law accepted completely the futility of the review when a detective sergeant from the Regional Crime Squad seriously suggested that the bank robbery had been Mafia inspired.

He sighed, allowing the meeting that had already lasted two hours to extend for a further fifteen minutes and then rose, ending it. He thanked them for their attendance, promised another discussion if there had been no break in the case within a fortnight and walked out of the room with Sergeant Hardiman.

'Waste of bloody time, that was,' he said, back in his office.

Hardiman waited at the door, accepting tea from the woman with the trolley.

'Bread pudding or Dundee cake?' asked the sergeant.

'Neither,' said Law.

Hardiman came carefully into the room, his pudding balanced on top of one of the cups.

'Mafia,' he echoed. 'Jesus Christ!'

'Funny though,' said Hardiman. He pushed an escaping crumb into his mouth.

'What is?'

'The dead end,' said the sergeant. 'We get the biggest job we've had in this manor for years. Indications of a professional safebreaker are everywhere and after almost a month, we've got nothing. No whispers, no gossip, no nothing.'

'So it was someone from outside. We decided that days ago,' Law reminded him. He had spoken too sharply, he realised.

'So who?' asked Hardiman, unoffended. 'Who, a stranger to the area, could set up a job like this?'

Law threw his hands up, wishing he'd accepted the bread

pudding. It looked very good and he'd only had a pickled egg and a pork pie for lunch, he remembered.

'It's in there, somewhere,' he said, gesturing towards the files stacked up against the wall. 'All we've got to do is find it.'

Hardiman carefully wiped the sugar from his lips and hands.

'That was nice; you should have had some,' said the sergeant. He looked towards the manila folders. 'It might be in there, but we're going to need help to see it.'

'One hundred and twenty boxes,' reflected Law. 'And carefully hidden in one of them was something that would make it all so clear to us.'

'But which one?' said Hardiman. 'We've interviewed the owners and they're all lying buggers.'

'Crime is not solved by brilliant intuition or startling intellect,' started Law, and Hardiman looked at him warily. The superintendent had a tendency to lecture, he thought.

' . . . it's solved by straightforward, routine police work,' completed Law. He looked expectantly at the other man.

When Hardiman said nothing, Law prompted. 'And what, sergeant, is the basis of routine police work?'

Hardiman still said nothing, aware of the other man's unhappiness at the lack of progress and unwilling to increase his anger with the wrong answer.

'Statements?' he tried at last.

Law smiled.

'Statements,' he agreed. 'Good, old-fashioned, copper-on-a-bike statements.'

Hardiman waited.

'So,' decided Law, 'we will start all over again. We'll turn out those bright sods who spend all their time watching television and admiring the Mafia and we'll go to every box-holder and we'll take a completely fresh statement, saying there are some additional points we want covered.' And then we'll practise straightforward, routine police work and compare everything they said first time with everything they say the second time. And where the difference is too great we'll go back again and take a third statement and if necessary a fourth and we'll keep on until we shake the bloody clue out of the woodwork.'

'It'll take a while,' warned Hardiman, doubtfully. 'That scruffy bloke with the home in Switzerland, for instance. The one we saw last? Telephoned yesterday to say he'd be in London for at least a week, on business.'

'Don't care how long it takes,' said Law positively. 'I want it done. If he's not back in a week contact that firm he gave us and get him back. I want everyone seen again. Everyone.'

'Right,' said Hardiman, moving out of the room. Law called, stopping him at the door.

'If you pass that tea-lady and she's still got some of that bread pudding, send her back with some, will you?'

'Certainly,' said the sergeant. There wouldn't be, he knew. He'd had the last piece. But the superintendent was annoyed enough as it was, so it was better not to tell him.

Edith left the Zürich apartment early, changing trains at Berne to catch the express. She crossed from Calais to Dover and hired a Jaguar, deciding the need for comfort during the amount of driving she might have to do justified the expense.

It was a bright, sharp day, the February sunshine too weak to take the overnight whiteness from the fields and hedges of Kent. She drove unhurriedly, cocooned in the warmth of the car, missing the worst of the traffic by skirting London to the west.

She got a room without difficulty at the Randolph and by eight o'clock was in the bar, with a sherry she didn't want, selecting a meal she knew she wouldn't enjoy.

'Scotch,' ordered Ruttgers, at the other end of the bar. 'Plenty of ice.'

TWENTY-ONE

The man was irritable, decided Johnny. And for the first time he did not appear completely sure of himself. Nervous, almost. The bigger surprise, determined the safebreaker. Because there definitely wasn't any cause for uncertainty. It had all gone like clockwork, just like the other two. Easier, in fact. Far easier. No dusty, gritty air-conditioning tubes. Or shitty drains. Just a simple entry through the back of the adjoining premises, a quick walk through the antique furniture all marked up at three times its price for the oil-rich Arabs and a neat little hole by the fireplace to bring them right into the main working area.

'Never been into a private bank before,' said Johnny, chattily. 'Very posh.'

'Doesn't seem as if they expected anyone to. Not at night, anyway,' said Snare, straightening up from the alarm system. He hadn't believed the plans Wilberforce had given him three hours before.

'What do you mean?' said Johnny.

Snare reached into the bag, bringing up the aerosol tube of tile fixative and squirting it liberally into the control box, sealing the hammers of the alarms.

'Must be fifteen years old,' he judged. 'They probably still count with an abacus.'

'Probably,' concurred Johnny, who didn't know what an abacus was. The other man was definitely friendlier, he decided happily.

They found a pressure pad beneath the carpet in the manager's office, three more behind junior executive desks and an electrical eye circuit, triggered when the beam was interrupted, in front of the strongroom and the safety deposit vault.

They were all governed by a control box it took them fifteen minutes to locate in the basement.

'Kid's stuff?' ventured Johnny hopefully.

'Kid's stuff,' agreed Snare.

'Can't beat a sock or a biscuit tin in the garden, can you?' continued Johnny, as the man immobilised the second system.

Snare grunted, without replying. He'd enjoy seeing this cocky little sod in the dock of the Old Bailey, he decided, trying to talk his way out of a fifteen-year sentence. Where, he wondered, would all the bombast and the boasting be then? Where his brains were, he decided. In his silk jockstrap, as useless as everything else.

'At this rate,' said Johnny, 'we'll be able to retire by the end of the year.'

'Maybe sooner,' said Snare, with feeling. Whatever happened, he determined, positively, this would be the last time. No matter how easy they made it for him, with all the plans and wiring systems drawings, it was still dangerous. And he'd suffered enough. Too much. Didn't he still need special pills, for the headaches? And they'd become more frequent in the last month. Like everything else, something that Wilberforce found easy to forget, in his anxiety to get his head off the block. He wasn't any more considerate than Cuthbertson. Worse even.

'Let's get started,' he said.

It took Johnny longer than they expected to open the safe in the manager's office and then Snare wasn't satisfied with the list of safe deposit box numbers he got from the top shelf.

'Nothing entered since last week,' he said almost to himself.

'What does that matter?'

'Try the desk.'

That was easier and it was there that Snare found the listing for Charlie.

'Conceited bastard,' he said, again a private remark. 'The conceited bastard.'

'What?'

Things were very different tonight, decided Johnny. Odd, in fact. It was making him feel uncomfortable.

'Nothing,' said Snare. As he had at the Savoy, Charlie had opened an account under his own name.

To get into the safety deposit vault, Johnny drilled out the lock on the protective gate and then filled three holes bored around the safe handle with P-4 to blow a hole big enough to reach inside and manually bring the time clock forward twelve hours, to open the door.

Inside the deposit room, Johnny worked with his steel wire, fashioning the skeleton keys as he worked, giving a little laugh at his own cleverness every time a tray snapped clear and came out on its runners.

'Lot of documents,' complained the crook.

'Perhaps that's why they don't bother too much with alarms.'

Snare allowed twelve boxes to be opened before he said, 'Now 48.'

Obediently Johnny hunched over the container, probing and poking. As the lock clicked back, Snare announced, 'I'll do this one.'

Johnny stepped aside, frowning. Definitely unsure of himself, judged Johnny again. He'd built up a conviction about the other man's infallibility, like a child believing the perfection of a sand sculpture. Now the tide was coming in and Johnny didn't like to see his imagery crumbling.

Snare was standing up in front of the box, staring down fixedly at a single piece of paper he'd taken from the tray.

'Any good?' enquired Johnny.

The other man looked at him unseeingly.

'Any good?' repeated the safebreaker.

Snare blinked, like a man awakening.

'Let's get out,' he said.

Johnny stared at him, his own doubts hardening.

'But we've only just begun . . . there's dozens more . . . thousands of pounds . . .'

'Finished,' ruled Snare, abrupt now but completely recovered. 'We've got enough.'

He mirrored Johnny's look, challengingly.

The safebreaker moved from foot to foot, unsure whether to argue. Finally he spread his hands, overly dismissive.

'Whatever you say,' he agreed. Stupid to spoil the arrangement by appearing greedy. They still hadn't agreed a price with the insurers yet on the Russian stuff and he didn't want to risk that.

Snare went first through the hole, leading back into the antique shop.

'You know what?' said Johnny, trying to reduce the strain and at the same time build up the relationship he was sure he could establish.

'What?'

'I don't know where your information comes from,' said Johnny. 'Don't want to, not necessarily. But I don't reckon we can ever lose. No way.'

Snare's apprehensive anger at everything spilled over and he rounded on the safebreaker, face tight so that the scar was etched out vividly.

'Sometimes,' he said, 'you piss me off.'

'What?' tried Johnny, backing away from the assault.

'Because you're full of piss,' shouted Snare wildly, finding release in the role of the bully. 'Full of piss.'

'You're fucking mad,' said Johnny, trying to match the obscenity. 'Absolutely fucking mad.'

Snare stopped the attack, taking the other man's words.

'You could be right,' he said, quietly now. 'That's the trouble; you could well be right.'

'Wanker,' said Johnny, made miserable by the collapse of yet another relationship.

Charlie, to whom the isolation of detail was automatic, had recognised Snare from his walk the moment the man had left the car and made his way towards the rear of the antique shop. And there he was again, he saw, as Snare left the rear of the building and approached the carefully parked station-wagon. Still the same shoulder-jogging lilt he'd had when he'd strode away in East Berlin, to set the tripwire for the ambush.

'Like a duck with a frozen bum,' Charlie told himself, inside the darkened car. The cold had occupied Charlie's mind for the last two nights. It was going to be a bad winter, he had decided.

Unspeaking, the two men entered Snare's car. There was a momentary pause and in the darkness Charlie could see Snare putting on his safety belt. Probably too late for that, thought Charlie. Snare's presence had surprised him.

Snare started the car and moved away slowly and almost immediately Charlie pulled out, holding back until they came out alongside the Playboy Club and two cars had intruded themselves between him and the station-wagon, a barrier of protection.

'As Wilberforce might say, the hunted becomes the hunter,' he muttered, trying to mock the man's speech. 'Now all you've got to do is to catch the bloody fox.'

'They've been very smart,' said Berenkov, admiringly.

'Yes,' agreed Kalenin. 'Very smart indeed.'

He smiled across the table at Valentina.

'After meals like that, I know I'm a fool to have remained a bachelor,' he praised her.

The plump woman flushed at the compliment and continued clearing the table.

'What can you do?'

Kalenin jerked his shoulders.

'Nothing,' he said. 'To make anything more than diplomatic protests would show them we've discovered Charlie's association with one of the insurers and allow the satisfaction of knowing we won't be laughing at them any more.'

'They'll know that anyway,' argued Berenkov. 'That's what it's all about.'

'We still can't admit it,' said Kalenin.

'What about Charlie?'

Again the K.G.B. chief moved uncertainly.

'Wouldn't it be marvellous if Charlie were to win?' suggested Berenkov, expansively.

'Marvellous,' agreed Kalenin, wondering at the amount of wine his friend had consumed. 'But quite unlikely.'

TWENTY-TWO

Charlie drove quite relaxed, allowing another vehicle to come between him and the car he was pursuing, so that when it turned unexpectedly to go down Constitution Hill he was able to follow quite naturally, without any sudden braking which might have sounded to attract the attention of Snare.

Only after they had gone around the Victoria monument in front of Buckingham Palace did Charlie close up, not wanting to be left behind at the traffic lights in Parliament Square. The second set were red. Through the glass of the one separating car, Charlie could see Snare and the other man stiffly upright and apparently not talking.

'Always an unfriendly sod,' remembered Charlie.

They went across Westminster Bridge and entered the one-way system. The sudden turn beneath the railway arch, to go into Waterloo station, almost took Charlie by surprise. He only just managed to swerve without tyre squeal, continuing slowly up the long approach and trying to keep a taxi between them. He stopped before the corner, for more taxis to overtake and provide a barrier, so that when he drove into the better-lighted part of the concourse, Snare was already moving off.

Charlie didn't hurry, wanting to see the car to which the second man went. Parked as it was, the vehicle was obviously not stolen but belonged to him. So he could get the man's name from the registration.

He went slowly by, memorising the number as he passed, finally speeding up to get into position behind Snare again.

Snare was driving very precisely, Charlie saw, giving every signal and keeping within the speed limit. Rules and regulations, recalled Charlie; the dictum of Snare's life. Without guidelines to keep within and precedents to follow, Snare had always been uncomfortable. Robbing banks, an open criminal activity, would have been difficult for him, even with the back-up and assistance provided by the department. On the occasions when he'd had to do it, he'd rather enjoyed it, thought Charlie. It was like playing roulette and knowing the ball would always fall on your number. But Snare would have hated it. The word stayed in Charlie's mind; the emotion that would have provided the necessary incentive, he supposed.

'He really can't have liked me very much,' Charlie smiled to himself. The expression left his face. There couldn't have been anything very amusing about Snare's Moscow imprisonment, admitted Charlie. Immediately he balanced the self-criticism. Just as there wasn't anything amusing at being chosen for assassination at a border crossing; he had no reason to feel guilt over the man in front. Snare's inability to adjust to the unexpected intruded into his mind. It made the outcome of tonight's journey almost predictable, he thought; Snare was an advantage he hadn't expected.

They went around Parliament Square but Snare kept to the south side of Buckingham Palace this time, heading into Pimlico. Traffic thinned as they entered the residential area and Charlie pulled back, losing his cover.

He stopped completely when he saw the tail-lights in front disappear to the left, into an enclosed square. He walked unhurriedly to the side road. The car was halfway along, neatly positioned in its residents' parking area, the permit prominently displayed. Snare was the sort of man to keep a cinema ticket in his pocket, in case he was challenged coming back from a pee during the interval, thought Charlie.

He waited until he saw the ground-floor lights go on, then returned to the car. He drove into the side road, but continued past Snare's home, going almost around the tiny park upon which the tall Regency buildings fronted. He stopped opposite Snare's house, but with the park between them, knowing he was completely concealed.

'How long?' wondered Charlie aloud.

It was nearly an hour. Charlie was beginning to fear he had miscalculated Snare's reaction when the light at which he was staring fixedly suddenly went out and then, seconds later, the door of the house opened. There was the delay while Snare fixed the safety belt and then the car moved off, circling behind to pass within feet of where Charlie waited. He gazed openly through the shaded glass, knowing he would be invisible to the other man. Snare drove bent slightly forward, away from the seat. His back would ache after long journeys, decided Charlie, allowing the man to turn out on to the main road before restarting the engine and pulling out to follow. Even in the darkened car, he had been able to see the scar disfiguring Snare's face. Charlie wondered how it had happened.

They went directly south, crossing the river over Chelsea Bridge and then, gradually, began taking the roads that would give them a route eastwards.

'So it *is* Wilberforce,' said Charlie. 'And he still lives at Tenterden.'

He had been to the man's country home once, Charlie remembered. It had been within a month of Cuthbertson's appointment and Wilberforce, ass-hole crawling as always, had thrown a party. His role had been that of the jester, recalled Charlie, paraded as a reminder of the stupid anachronisms that Cuthbertson and his team of bright young university-educated, army-trained recruits were going to revitalise. He'd got drunk and told Wilberforce's wife an obscene story about a short-sighted showgirl and a donkey, expecting her to be shocked. Instead she had started to squeeze his hand and kept asking him to open bottles of a rather inferior Piesporter Goldtropfchen for her, in the kitchen. Should have given her a quick knee-trembler, over the draining board, decided Charlie, in belated regret. She'd worn corsets, though, with little dangly things to support her stockings. And Wilberforce had kept appearing, as if he'd realised the danger.

Even on an open road and as confused as Charlie expected him to be, Snare wasn't exceeding fifty miles an hour. A fact to remember, decided Charlie. Timing the other man was going to be important tonight.

Because Snare was establishing the speed, it took them almost two hours to reach the Kent village. Impatient now and quite sure of the other man's destination, Charlie didn't bother to see him actually enter the drive of Wilberforce's house.

Instead he made a wide loop at the crossroads, hurrying through the gears to pick up speed and rejoin the road to London.

Three hours to achieve what he wanted, Charlie estimated, smiling at the burbling of the widened exhaust. Sounded like Cuthbertson, he thought, just before one of those filthy coughs he was always making. Charlie laughed aloud, extending the thought. Christ, how Cuthbertson would have choked if he had been in a position to know what was going to happen.

Ruttgers sprawled full length on the coverlet of the hotel bedroom, telephone cupped loosely to his ear, enjoying the admission from the man who had replaced him.

'Quite obvious,' Onslow Smith repeated. 'A meeting between them can be the only point.'

'And we're handling it this time,' Ruttgers reminded him. 'No more foul-ups by the British.'

He'd made a dirty mark on the counterpane, he saw; he should have taken his shoes off.

'I'm thinking of discussing the whole thing with the Secretary of State,' announced Smith.

'He won't like it.'

'He'll like it less if something happens and he's not been warned.'

'Why not wait? We could have the whole thing buttoned up in a day or two.'

'Maybe,' conceded Smith. Thank God he had his own people in Ruttger's support team, to warn him the moment there was any sign of Charlie Muffin. Increasingly Smith was coming to think that Ruttgers saw the whole thing as a personal vendetta, like some Western shoot-out at high noon. He suspected the man didn't give a damn about the Agency any more.

'I want you to be careful, Garson,' he warned. 'Very careful indeed.'

'I will be.'

It was too quick, judged Smith. Dismissive almost.

'I mean it,' insisted the Director. 'There must be no chance of our being identified.'

'Don't worry,' said Ruttgers.

'I *do* worry,' said Smith. 'This whole thing is coming unglued.'

'I'll keep in touch,' promised Ruttgers, swinging his legs off the bed to search for a replacement cigarette. 'Nothing will go wrong.'

'That's what Wilberforce was saying, a week ago.'

'What was in the private bank, by the way?' enquired Ruttgers, locating a fresh pack of cigarettes.

'Snare only went in tonight,' Smith replied. 'I haven't heard yet.'

Wilberforce's dressing gown was very long and full-skirted and made swishing sounds as he strode about the study. Snare sat uneasily on the edge of the chair by the desk, eager for some guidance from his superior.

'I thought you should see it, right away,' he said, almost in apology.

'Quite right,' said Wilberforce absently. 'Quite right.'

He paused before a small side table on which drinks were arranged, then appeared to change his mind, returning to the desk.

'What does it mean?' asked Snare.

Wilberforce picked up a piece of paper that Snare had

taken from the Mayfair safe deposit box and stared down at it, shaking his head.

'God knows,' he said. Concern was marked in his voice.

He threw it aside, and Snare retrieved it, examining it with the same intensity as the other man. ' ... "Clap hands, here comes Charlie"' he recited. He looked back to Wilberforce.

'It's like some sort of challenge, isn't it?' he said.

'Yes,' agreed Wilberforce miserably, 'it's a challenge.'

At that moment, fifty miles farther north, Charlie Muffin eased a plastic credit card through a basement window, prodded the catch up and two minutes later was standing in the darkened kitchen of Snare's Pimlico home. Funny, decided Charlie, after all that Snare had been up to in the last few weeks and there wasn't the slightest attempt at security in his own house. Still, he reflected, the attitude was typical. People always expected misfortune to occur to someone else, never themselves. Carefully he refastened the window and began walking towards the stairs leading upwards. He sniffed, appreciatively. Remains of the last meal still smelt good. Curry, he decided. He wouldn't have imagined Snare had had time to cook. Probably out of a packet. Remarkable, the value available in supermarkets these days.

TWENTY-THREE

Charlie worked expertly and very quickly. He had been diligently trained by a housebreaker who earned the wartime amnesty for past misdeeds by being parachuted on three separate occasions into Nazi-occupied France and Holland and then stayed on Home Office attachment in peacetime, lecturing on the finer points of his craft to police forces throughout the country.

On the ground floor he moved immediately to the rear,

where a door opened on to a small, paved patio and the darkened garden beyond. He opened it, testing to ensure it would not close by its own weight. Satisfied that he had an escape route if the need suddenly arose, he went back into the house, swiftly checking each room in turn, then slowly climbed the stairs, listening for·any faint sound of occupation and more carefully now examined the bedrooms. Each was empty. From his examination of the outside, while he had been waiting for Snare earlier in the evening, he knew there was a third storey. He located the stairway at the back of the house and carried out the same precautions in the rooms there. Empty again.

'Charlie,' he said, 'the stars shine upon you.'

And it was about bloody time, he thought.

On the ground floor he began making a detailed search of every room. It was a neat, antiseptically clean house, the furniture and pictures and ornaments arranged more as if for a photograph in a good housekeeping magazine than for living amongst and enjoying. Making constant reference to the time and alert for any sound outside the house that might warn of Snare's return, Charlie still handled everything cautiously, returning every picture and the contents of every drawer or cupboard to exactly the position he had found it, so his entry would not be instantly apparent.

The study was at the back of the house, overlooking the patio, and Charlie checked all the pictures or wall-covering pieces of furniture intently, seeking the safe. After fifteen minutes, he perched contemplatively on the edge of the desk, frowning. Surely Snare would have a safe? Perhaps the stars weren't as bright as he had imagined. He re-checked, still found nothing, and even probed beneath the carpet, in case it were floor mounted.

Finally accepting there was no such installation in the room, Charlie turned to the desk. The working place of an orderly, rules-and-regulations man, Charlie decided. The bills in the top drawer were arranged and catalogued for dates of payment. Letters awaiting reply were in the drawer below, also catalogued, and those answered filed with their carbon copies in the one below that. The files were in the deepest shelf, at the very bottom. Charlie started expectantly, but immediately realised there were just household records; Snare actually kept a detailed account book for the car, he saw. Even the amount spent on petrol was carefully listed.

'Mean bugger,' judged Charlie.

He found the keys in the left-hand top drawer in which there was a partitioned shelf with small containers. Charlie stared down at them. A man as neat as Snare would arrange them in order of importance, he decided. There were duplicates of house, car and Automobile Association keys and in another tray were what appeared spare sets for luggage or a briefcase. That left four for which there was no obvious identification. They were in the first container.

Charlie quickly tried the remaining drawers, expecting to find at least one of them locked, but all opened smoothly to his touch.

Charlie left the room and started the search of the first floor. It was easier here, because there was less furniture. In two of the bedrooms, it was actually protected by dust-sheets. Snare's bedroom was as neat as the study, the shoes not only in racks but enclosed in tiny plastic bags and the clothes carefully arranged in a wardrobe like a colour chart, running from pale, summer-weight material through to the darker, heavier suits.

'Housemaster would be very proud of you,' said Charlie.

He found the locked cupboard on the floor above and sighed, relieved. It was specially made, he saw, the doors flush and with two locks, top and bottom. He pulled at the handle. There was no movement. So it was rigid-frame, too. Probably steel.

It took less than a minute to return from the study with the unidentifiable keys. The second fitted the bottom lock and when he retried the first, the top clicked back into place.

Charlie edged away, pulling open the door, and then sighed in open astonishment.

'Oh, the fools,' he said. 'The bloody fools.'

The Fabergé collection was laid out almost as if for inspection, arranged on three shelves. On the floor beneath were the plastic bags in which Snare and Johnny had carried it from the gallery.

The whole point of the entry had been to find something – anything – with which he might have been able to incriminate Snare; a plan of the Brighton bank, for instance. Or maybe some connection with the Tate. But not this. Not the single most damning thing there could possibly be.

Of course the proceeds of the robbery could not have been openly taken into the department, accepted Charlie. But Snare should and could have made his own security arrangements; he'd been inside enough banks in the last month to be a bloody expert. His judgment of those who had taken over the department from Sir Archibald and even survived the Kalenin affair wasn't, as Edith suspected and of which she had accused him, the biased sniping of someone who had been dismissed as unnecessary, thought Charlie. They *were* amateurs, like the men who could not accept that Kim Philby was a spy because he'd been to the right school or that there was a risk in Guy Burgess, boozing and male-whoring in every embassy to which he'd been attached.

He packed the jewellery, relocked the cupboard and returned the keys to the desk. He spent fifteen minutes assuring himself that he had replaced everything in the position from which it had originally been moved, then a further ten in one of the spare, unused bedrooms.

Finally he went out the back door, quietly pulling it closed after him, climbed easily over the separating fence at the bottom of the garden and then out through the front gate of the neighbouring house on to the road parallel to that in which Snare lived.

The car was still warm from the drive back from Kent, he found, pausing gratefully before starting the engine.

'You're a lucky sod, Charlie,' he told himself.

*

'What about the safebreaker?' suggested Cuthbertson, matching everyone else's desperation. 'Perhaps he followed Snare home?'

Onslow Smith sighed at the confusion that had grown in Wilberforce's office since his entry.

'Oh come on!' he said, rejecting the idea. 'This is stupid, panic thinking.'

And there was damned good reason to panic, he thought. If he weren't very careful, this would make the Bay of Pigs and the Allende overthrow in Chile look like a training exercise for Boy Scouts. Which, upon examination, seemed about its right level.

'It's a possibility,' Cuthbertson said defensively, his thick voice showing he knew it was nothing of the sort.

The American picked up the note that had been taken from the Mayfair bank.

'That's rubbish and you know it,' he said, waving the paper towards the ex-Director. 'We've been suckered. Well and truly suckered.'

'Personal animosity isn't going to help,' said Wilberforce, trying to reduce the tension. It had been impossible to sleep after Snare's visit the previous night and the hollow feeling that had gouged out his stomach at the man's breakfast telephone call, reporting that the collection was missing, had developed into positive nausea. He'd even tried to be sick, thrusting his finger down his throat in the bathroom adjoining his office, and merely made himself feel worse.

'I don't know what will,' said Smith. 'I can't believe it. I just can't believe that you didn't take any precautions. Jesus!'

'Would you have stored it in the American embassy?' threw back Wilberforce.

'No,' admitted Smith immediately. 'I'd have certainly put it in Snare's house. And then I'd have made damned sure that there were so many people watching that house that a kitchen mouse couldn't have taken a pee without someone knowing it.'

He was going to get out, decided Smith, suddenly. He was

going to withdraw all his men and get to hell out of it, before the smell really started to rise. From now on, Wilberforce was where he'd always wanted to be. On his own.

'I made a mistake,' conceded Wilberforce, reluctantly. 'I'm very sorry.'

The other Director looked crushed, thought Smith, without any pity.

'Does anyone in your government know what's been going on?' he asked.

'No,' said Wilberforce. 'And yours?'

'No.'

'It'll be a miracle if it remains a secret,' said Wilberforce.

'It is quite obvious that Charlie has taken it,' said Braley.

'To return to the insurers?' queried Cuthbertson.

Wilberforce nodded at the question. 'Equally obvious,' he said. 'It's the only way he could ensure that Rupert Willoughby wouldn't be damaged by association. Don't forget how close he was to Sir Archibald.'

Wilberforce laid aside his worry pipe, looking across the desk encouragingly.

'The Fabergé collection was always intended to be returned to the Russians, which is now what will undoubtedly happen. So the damage at the moment is still minimal.'

'But we don't know where the hell Charlie Muffin is,' said Snare.

'But we know *how* to re-locate him,' said Wilberforce. 'There's got to be some sort of pattern in the woman's tour. The moment there is any contact, we'll have him again.'

Smith decided he'd wait until he organised the removal of his own men before letting Wilberforce know what he was doing. Then the son of a bitch could do what he wanted about watching Edith.

'I'd like to think so,' said Snare. He felt revulsed that Charlie Muffin had entered his home and actually touched things that he owned. Quite often, he recalled, the man hadn't bathed every day.

'Where's the flaw?' demanded Wilberforce. No one guessed the depths of his uncertainty, he knew.

Smith shook his head at the other man's stupidity.

'The flaw,' he said, patiently, 'is what it's always been – Charlie Muffin.'

TWENTY-FOUR

Quite irrationally, which she even recognised but still could not prevent, Edith had developed a conviction that despite the lengthy list of cities and hotels that Charlie had given, he would have contacted her almost immediately.

She'd actually invoked ridiculous, childlike rituals. If the waiter at dinner were Spanish, then Charlie would telephone before midnight. If the winter coldness broke, turning to rain, then that would be the day she would walk into the car park and find Charlie waiting for her.

The desperation had grown with each day until that morning, just before leaving her Cambridge hotel and starting the drive southward to Crawley, the next town designated, she had had to hold herself rigidly at the bedroom door, fighting against the overwhelming impulse to cry.

That it should happen there, today, was understandable, she supposed. She had read history at Girton and the memories had soaked through her. She had driven along the Huntingdon Road and gazed in, trying to locate her old room. And walked past King's Chapel, so that she could stand on the tiny, humped bridge to stare down into the icy water of the Backs, too cold even for the ducks, and remember the summer punting of so long ago. And smiled reminiscently at the couples, encompassed in their scarves and undergraduate romances, and envied them their happiness.

And now she was going back to Sussex, which she had already come to hate, even before Charlie had made the drunken mistake there that had begun all the agony. Then again, she thought, her mind slipping away on a familiar path, perhaps it was an omen; perhaps it would be here that it would end, where it had begun. That was it; had to be. Charlie would appear today, with the shy yet cocky I-told-you-so smile that always came when he'd proved himself right, and explain how he'd fooled everyone and they could clear out forever, burying themselves in Switzerland again.

She felt the panic building up and gripped the wheel. Just like the Spanish waiters and the weather, she thought, angrily. Damned ridiculous. Why couldn't she accept it? Charlie wouldn't come. Today. Or any other day. It would be a month of aimless journeyings to towns she didn't want to see until one day there would be a telephone call from Rupert Willoughby, a man she'd never met and probably never would, trying to infuse the proper melancholy into his voice to tell her that Charlie, who had forgotten to kiss her when he left that day in Zürich, hadn't been clever enough this time and was dead.

She pulled the car into a layby, trying to blink the emotion away. She had to stop it, she knew. She was collapsing under the weight of her own self-induced fear. And Charlie wanted her help, not her collapse. She found it so difficult.

Recovered, she felt her way back into the traffic and reached the timbered George Hotel just before lunch. Despite the determination in the layby, she still searched hopefully around the car park as she pulled in, then again in the foyer as she registered. With difficulty, she focused on the receptionist, realising the girl was repeating a question.

'I wondered if you would want lunch?'

'No,' said Edith, too sharply. 'No thank you,' she repeated, embarrassed at her own rudeness.

'Is anything the matter, madam?'

'Long drive,' stumbled Edith. 'Rather tired.'

She didn't bother to unpack the suitcases. Instead she stood at the window of her room, staring down unseeingly into Crawley High Street.

'Hurry up, Charlie,' she said softly. 'I need you so very much.'

In the lobby below, the polite receptionist was dealing with an unexpected influx of guests. It was fortunate, she thought, that it was so early in the season, otherwise she would have had difficulty in finding accommodation for them all. There were no wives, so it must be a business conference, she decided. Unusual that she hadn't heard about it. Probably in Brighton.

And in that town, just twenty miles to the south, Superintendent Law was summoning the sergeant for the second conference of the day.

'Well?' demanded the superintendent.

Hardiman shook his head, indicating the files banked up against the wall.

'Still got about twenty more statements to repeat,' he said. 'But so far there's nothing.'

'It must be there somewhere,' said Law, refusing to admit his idea was wrong.

Then you're the best bugger to find it, thought the sergeant.

'Odd overnight report,' he said, trying to move the superintendent past his fixation with the statements.

'What?'

'You know we asked the uniformed branch to keep an eye on that financier's house?'

Law nodded.

'Copper on last night hadn't done it before,' continued Hardiman. 'Got the impression that there was some sort of separate observation being carried out ... mentioned it to his superintendent in case there had been some confusion and we were duplicating...'

'What about the other policemen, before him?' demanded Law instantly.

'I've checked,' said the sergeant, glad he'd anticipated the request. 'Two others got the same impression. Didn't mention it because they thought we *were* doubling up.'

'Stupid bastards,' said Law. 'Have we interviewed him again?'

Hardiman shook his head.

'Away on business,' he reminded him. 'Took the trouble to telephone us.'

He picked up Charlie's file and the superintendent took it from him, staring down as if he expected a clue he hadn't appreciated from the statement suddenly to present itself.

'It's not much,' said the sergeant, concerned at the other man's interest. He hoped Law wouldn't get too worked up. The constable's report hadn't been made overnight. It had been lying around for two days, but Hardiman had forgotten to mention it.

'Willoughby, Price and Rowledge,' Law read from the file.

'They've confirmed his association with them,' said Hardiman. 'Shall I contact them again?'

Hurriedly Law shook his head.

'Mustn't frighten the rabbit,' he said.

'What then?' asked Hardiman. It was almost impossible to guess which way the superintendent's mind would jump, he thought, annoyed.

'Let's try to find out a bit more about him first,' suggested Law. He paused and the sergeant waited, knowing he hadn't finished.

'Remember what he said that first night, when we went to his house?' prompted Law.

Hardiman looked doubtful.

'Made some remark about being a financier, even though his passport described him as a clerk.'

'Why should that be odd?' asked Hardiman.

'I don't know, laddie. I don't know,' said the superintendent, patronisingly. 'Why don't we check the passport office, to discover if it is?'

Why did Law have to conduct everything like it was a sodding quiz game? wondered Hardiman, walking towards his own office. Sometimes the man really pissed him off.

Involvement had been thrust upon Willoughby and Charlie had anticipated the reluctance that was becoming obvious. He hadn't expected the underwriter's argument against the stupidity of vindictiveness. That had surprised him.

To Willoughby, of course, the two were so interlinked as to be practically the same. But to Charlie, they were quite separate. To beat them, as he knew he now had, as well as surviving, had more than justified any risk. And there hadn't been any; not much, anyway. Almost like rigged roulette, again. Now it was over. And he'd got away with it.

Momentarily he looked away from his search for the turning off Wimbledon Hill Road that Willoughby had named during their argumentative conversation, checking the time. Almost midnight; everything would have happened by this time tomorrow, he thought.

He'd been very fortunate, Charlie thought. The confidence bubbled up. But he'd been clever enough to seize that good fortune and utilise it. Christ, how he'd utilised it.

Despite the force of a Lloyd's insurers behind it, he had still been surprised at the speed with which Willoughby had obtained John Packer's address from the car registration. The house was at the bottom of a cul-de-sac, a horseshoe indentation between two major roads. Charlie didn't stop, driving out on to the avenue that backed on to Packer's property, counting along until he isolated the house between him and the one he was seeking. He parked the car, entered through a tree-lined drive, skirted the darkened building and then smiled, with growing awareness, at the lowness of the fence between it and Packer's home. The separation between the other adjoining property, from which it would be possible to reach the alternative main road, would be similarly low, he guessed.

Charlie realised almost immediately that he would not be able easily to enter the house. Inside each of the lower windows there was actually a reinforced mesh clamped into a separate frame to form a positive barrier, in addition to the special window locks and the small steel bolts that had been fitted in each corner. With such precautions, it was pointless trying the doors, Charlie decided.

'Pity a few other people hadn't been as cautious as you, Mr Packer,' muttered Charlie.

At first Charlie thought the shed might have been built

over an old coal-chute, by which he might still have been able to get in, through the cellar. Obedient to his training, he remained unmoving immediately inside the door, first feeling out for any obstruction and then, careful to avoid the reflection showing through the side windows, probing with the pencil-beam torch.

It wasn't until he'd shifted the sodium chlorate aside, thinking first of its gardening use, and discovered what lay behind that he appreciated its proper significance, squatting before it and all the other explosives, then moving up to the shelves to feel through the detonators and fuses and finally examining the box containing the timing and pressure devices. There were even clocks, to activate them.

'A regular little bomb factory,' mused Charlie. 'So you're the professional, Mr Packer? The one who's necessary to make it look right.'

It was the confirmation of the impression that had come to him climbing over the garden fence; the house was ideally positioned, with three easy escape routes against arrest.

Charlie extinguished the torch, re-locked the outhouse and left the garden by the route he had entered. The man had been manipulated enough, he decided.

TWENTY-FIVE

The arrests on the day that George Wilberforce was later to regard as the worst in his life should have been perfectly co-ordinated, but inevitably there was a mistake.

The information had identified the Kent house and the assumption of the Flying Squad and the Regional Crime Squad was that Wilberforce would be there as well. But it was a week-day and so he was staying in the Eaton Square apartment.

The superintendent who had liaised between the two forces and organised the raid went with just two cars to

London, leaving the main police contingent at Tenterden, with instructions to the women police officers that the woman bordering on hysteria should in no circumstances be allowed near a telephone.

During the drive through the early morning traffic they heard by radio that the seizure of Brian Snare had gone perfectly. The man had answered the door in his dressing gown, eyes widening in surprise at the number of police cars effectively sealing the Pimlico square, and was still spluttering his protests when they had found some jewelled eggs and the orb from the Fabergé collection hidden in the spare bedroom of the house.

Wilberforce was dressed when the squad arrived and his reaction was more controlled than they had expected. They refused his demand to use a telephone and when he had tried to insist upon his legal rights, an inspector said 'Bollocks' and the superintendent nodded in agreement.

They had left London before Wilberforce spoke again.

'This is a very big mistake,' he said.

The superintendent sighed. 'I'd like ten pounds for every time I've been told that as I've got my hand on a collar,' he said. He spoke across Wilberforce, as though the man were quite unimportant.

'Me too,' said the inspector.

'I'll want your names,' blustered Wilberforce.

'Here we go,' said the inspector. 'Bet he knows the commander.'

'I do,' insisted Wilberforce.

'The names,' said the superintendent, bored with the familiar charade, 'are Superintendent Hebson and Inspector Burt. We do have warrant cards, if you'd care to see them.'

'I shall hold you personally responsible if the men you've left behind at my flat cause any damage,' said Wilberforce.

'Of course,' agreed the superintendent. He was staring through the window, appearing more interested in the countryside.

'I'm still waiting for a satisfactory explanation,' said Wilberforce.

The superintendent remained gazing out of the window, so Inspector Burt turned, smiling over the back of the seat.

'We have reason to believe that you might have information to help us in our enquiries into the theft of the Fabergé collection which was on show at the Tate,' he said, formally.

'Oh, my God,' said Wilberforce.

Hebson turned back into the car at the remark.

'And it's still a big mistake, is it?' he said sarcastically.

'You don't understand,' said Wilberforce.

'Perhaps you'd like to explain it to me.'

The Director shook his head.

'You can't know,' he said, his voice still clouded. 'Oh, my God!'

The two policemen exchanged looks.

'We're going to, eventually,' Hebson assured him.

Again Wilberforce shook his head, but this time he turned to the policeman, struggling to compose himself.

'There must be no announcement about the recovery,' he said urgently. He gestured to the front of the car. 'Get on to the radio and say you want a complete publicity blackout.'

'There's to be no announcement, until we're sure we've got everything nicely stitched up,' guaranteed the superintendent, intrigued by the man's demeanour.

'Repeat it,' urged Wilberforce, reaching out and seizing the man's arm in his anxiety. 'I insist that you do.'

'At the moment,' Hebson reminded him, 'you're not in a position to insist upon anything, Mr Wilberforce.'

The policeman had allowed Wilberforce's wife to dress but she hadn't applied any make-up. She giggled when she saw her husband enter between the two officers, looking at him hopefully.

'What is it, George?' she demanded, shrilly. 'Where did all that jewellery come from?'

Hebson looked enquiringly at the inspector he had left in charge of the Tenterden house.

'In the cellar, sir,' reported the inspector. He nodded towards Wilberforce's wife. 'Says she knows nothing about it.'

'Where?' asked Wilberforce, dully.

He had expected the inspector to answer, but instead his wife replied, giggling as if inviting him to be as amused as she was.

'I'd even forgotten we had it,' she said. 'Do you remember that rather cheap Piesporter Goldtropfchen we got . . . must be years ago. It was behind there.'

'Shall we see?' invited Hebson.

Wilberforce led the way, shoulders sagged at the complete acceptance of what had happened. At the bottom of the cellar steps he stopped, uncertainly, so it was his wife who guided the party the last few yards towards an archway at the rear of the dank-smelling basement.

'There!' she announced. In her bewilderment she sounded proud.

The collection had been taken out of the plastic containers and laid out, almost for inspection. In the dull light from the unshaded bulbs, the diamonds, rubies and pearls glittered up, like the bright eyes of limp, unmoving animals.

The woman sniggered.

'Look,' she said, to her husband. 'Look at the way the long coach of that train has been arranged between those two Easter eggs . . .'

The laughter became more nervous.

' . . . it looks like . . . well, it's positively rude. . .'

Hebson looked painfully to the back of the group, to a policewoman.

'I think we're going to need a doctor soon,' he warned. He came back to Wilberforce. 'Well sir?' he said.

Wilberforce turned abruptly, trying to regain some command. He pointed to Hebson and Burt.

'My study,' he said.

He walked hurriedly back to the cellar steps, leaving his wife to the care of the policewoman.

'No doubt,' said Wilberforce, when the three of them had entered the room off the main hallway, 'you found similar jewellery in the home of a man called Brian Snare!'

'We did,' said Hebson, imagining the beginning of a confession.

'The bastard,' said Wilberforce, softly.

'Sir?' said Burt. He'd taken a notebook from his pocket.

Wilberforce straightened, fingers against the desk. Instinctively, he groped out, picking up a pipe but when he felt into his waistcoat he discovered that in the flurry from the Eaton Square apartment, he'd forgotten to take the tiny container of tools from the dressing table. He stared down at the pipe, as if it were important, then sadly replaced it in the rack.

'My name,' he announced, looking back to the men, 'is George Wilberforce . . .'

'We know that, sir,' said Hebson.

'And I am the Director of British Intelligence,' Wilberforce completed.

The confidence fell away from the two detectives like wind suddenly emptying from a sail.

'Oh,' said Hebson.

Wilberforce jerked his head towards the telephone.

'Call your commander,' he instructed. He took an address book from a desk drawer, selected a page and then offered it to the superintendent. 'And then the Prime Minister's office,' he added. 'That's the private number which will get you by the Downing Street exchange. I want his Personal Private Secretary, no one else.'

Hebson hesitated, finally taking the book. He began moving towards the telephone, but then turned to the inspector.

'Get on to one of the radios,' he ordered, indiciating the driveway outside. 'For Christ's sake screw the lid on this.'

Burt began moving.

' . . . and make sure we get a doctor for poor Mrs Wilberforce,' Hebson shouted after him.

The meeting with the Prime Minister took place the same

day. It was originally scheduled for the afternoon, but Smallwood postponed it twice, first for assurances from the Chief Constable of Kent and the Metropolitan Police Commissioner that the information could be suppressed and then because of an interview which the Russian ambassador suddenly requested with the Foreign Secretary. It was not until late into the evening that Wilberforce was finally shown into the study overlooking St James's Park. Smallwood sat behind the desk, stiff formality concealing his apprehension, well trained in the brutality of politics and moving quite calculatingly.

'There seems little point in saying how sorry I am,' said Wilberforce.

'None,' agreed the Premier.

'There were some miscalculations,' admitted the Director.

'About which I do not want to hear,' cut in Smallwood. 'You've been made to look ridiculous ... utterly ridiculous.'

'I realise that,' said Wilberforce.

'Over fifty policemen were involved in the raids upon you and that other damned man. Fifty policemen! Can you imagine that we're going to be able to stop something like this leaking out, with that many mouths involved?'

'We've still got the chance of locating him,' said Wilberforce, unthinkingly. 'The man responsible, I mean.'

'Mr Wilberforce,' said Smallwood, leaning forward on the desk and spacing the words for effect. 'I don't think you fully understand me. Or the point of this meeting. From this moment ... right at this moment ... the whole preposterous matter is concluded. There is to be no further action whatsoever. By anyone. Is that clear?'

The Director did not reply immediately and Smallwood thought he was going to argue.

At last he said: 'Quite clear.'

'Nothing,' retierated Smallwood. 'By anyone.'

'I see,' Wilberforce answered.

Silence came down like a partition between them.

'No,' said the Prime Minister. 'I still don't think you do.'

'Sir?' enquired Wilberforce.

Smallwood looked expectantly at him.

'Don't you have something to say to me?' he encouraged.

'Say to ...' started Wilberforce and then stopped, swallowing.

'Oh,' he said, comprehending.

'There can be no other course, surely?' said Smallwood. He wanted a scapegoat trussed and oven-ready. Several, in fact.

'I wish to offer my resignation,' said Wilberforce. He spoke mechanically, as if he were reading the words from a prepared speech. His hands moved, anxious for activity. He clasped them tightly in his lap.

'Thank you,' bustled the Premier. 'I accept. With regret, of course.'

'Of course.'

'It will have to be in writing,' said Smallwood.

'You'll have it by noon tomorrow,' promised Wilberforce.

'I'd like it earlier,' said Smallwood. 'Tonight.'

'But that's ...' Wilberforce began to protest, then saw the paper that the other man was offering. He scrawled his signature at the bottom of the already typed letter, not bothering to read it.

'Goodbye, Prime Minister,' said Wilberforce, striving for dignity.

'Goodbye,' said Smallwood.

He suddenly became occupied with some document on his desk and did not bother to look up as the man left the room.

'Every piece?' enquired Berenkov.

'Everything,' said Kalenin. 'All returned.'

The burly, white-haired Russian stood up and went to the window of Kalenin's office. The central heating was keeping the windows free from ice, but the snow was pouched on the roof-tops, like dirty white caps.

'That would mean they've finished with Charlie, then?'

'Yes,' agreed the K.G.B. officer.

'There haven't been any more leaks?'

'Not yet.'

'There would have been, surely?' said Berenkov, hope-fully.

'Alexei,' said Kalenin, kindly. 'He *must* be dead.'

'Yes,' Berenkov agreed. 'He must be.'

He turned into the room.

'At least the agony will be over for him,' he said.

TWENTY-SIX

Before assuming overall command of the Agency, Onslow Smith had been administrative director and it was with organisation that he felt happiest. He worked quickly and incisively in the room that had been set aside for him in the American embassy, the master set of papers immediately before him and the subsidiary files in an orderly arrangement at the top of the desk. Braley had arranged it all and done it well, considered Smith. If he could, he'd salvage Braley, he decided. He'd just have to be circumspect about it. And that was exactly what he was going to be about everything, thought Smith. Circumspect. Within twenty-four hours, every single operative involved in the Charlie Muffin fiasco would have been safely airlifted back to the protective anonymity of the C.I.A. headquarters in Virginia.

He looked up from the papers, stopped by a thought. And not one of them compromised. He looked back at the list of names before him, frowning at the number of operatives. All those men operating in the field, he thought. Damned near a miracle, he accepted. He extended the reflection, leaning back in his chair. One lucky; another one unlucky. Poor Wilberforce. He'd been so sure of himself.

And in the beginning, the idea had looked pretty good, conceded the American honestly. Dangerous, but still good. They'd just underestimated the victim.

He reached out, pulling a file nearer and then opened it at a picture of Charlie Muffin. He stared down at the image, running his finger along the edge of the photograph. Once, he remembered, the idea had been half-formed in his mind that perhaps he might possibly meet the man who had caused so much damage. But now it would never happen; Charlie would always remain a slightly out of focus impression and a bad memory. A very bad memory.

The telephone jarred into the room. The American Air Force transporter had arrived at London airport from Mildenhall; as they were being processed under diplomatic passports, bypassing completely the main passenger section and all the usual formalities, departure for Washington was scheduled within three hours.

Smith sighed, replacing the receiver. With a flourish betraying his rising confidence, he drew a line through the main list of operatives. Perfect, he decided. Like everything he organised.

Smith watched the seconds flicker by on the digital clock on the desk, waiting for ten o'clock to register. When it did, he put another line through the team that had been operatin Zürich. Because there were only five men, he'd felt it safe for them to fly direct from Switzerland to America on a scheduled flight: it was leaving on time, he knew from the confirmation he'd already received. So, too, were the couriers he had sent by road to ensure the withdrawal from the Brighton house and the Crawley hotel.

Charlie, who had been watching the George since just after dawn and had actually caught sight of Edith's drawn, unsmiling face through the breakfast room window, saw the messenger arrive and the trained attention to detail marked the significance.

'How many Ivy League suits are there in Crawley at this time of the year?' Charlie asked himself.

Quite a few, he thought, watching the sudden exodus of

men. The newcomer urged them into various cars, then pushed towards the driver of each an apparent written sheet of instructions. The newcomer left first, heading north. The other cars followed at five-minute intervals, to avoid attracting attention. Charlie waited until the last vehicle pulled out and then started his own engine.

'Better make sure,' he advised himself.

Once clear of the town, the cars had slowed, so by the time they reached the motorway, they were travelling in loose convoy. Charlie kept them comfortably in sight, glad of the flow of traffic he knew would conceal his pursuit.

It was not until they had continued past Gatwick airport, but then looped off, on to the Leatherhead road, to avoid the congestion of London to join the M-4, that Charlie realised they were heading for London airport, not the city. So the clothes *had* identified them as Americans. It had been a joint operation, he guessed, an operation being abandoned with all the panic that Willoughby had inferred at the strained meeting between the Russians and the government officials when the Fabergé collection had been returned. Now it was all over, the underwriter's attitude was changing again to friendship, he reflected.

Because of the increased volume of cars as they neared London airport, Charlie had to move closer than he really wanted, but it meant he was close enough not to be confused when, instead of becoming part of the crocodile slowly funnelling beneath the tunnel into the airport complex, the cavalcade swung off the roundabout and picked up one of the roads skirting the airport.

In a greater hurry than he had imagined, decided Charlie, slowing in recognition. They were going towards the north side of the airport, to the private section. The arrival had obviously been communicated ahead by radio in one of the cars. From the buildings swarmed not only airport security men, but American marines as well. They patterned out, sealing the area for a radius of three hundred yards.

Charlie pulled quickly into a car park reserved for the airport staff, then got out of the car, straining to focus the aircraft in the distance. He got final confirmation of the thoughts that had begun when he had seen the men move out of the hotel from the U.S. military plane drawn up close to one of the V.I.P. buildings, its dirty-khaki colouring merging with the surroundings.

He saw the cars stop and the occupants start to emerge, filing into one of the buildings. American military staff began loading the baggage directly into the aircraft hold.

'Complete diplomatic clearance,' mused Charlie, then stopped, identifying the figure in apparent command of the aircraft boarding.

So William Braley had been involved, as well as Snare. He smiled at the realisation; everyone who had had reason to hate him most. Good motivation, Charlie accepted.

He'd admired Braley, Charlie remembered. A complete and thorough professional. He was one of the people about whom Charlie felt most regret at what had happened in Vienna.

He sighed. A necessary casualty of survival, he decided. But still sad.

He got back into the mini and started back towards the roundabout from which he could rejoin the motorway.

'You did it, Charlie,' he congratulated himself. 'You beat them.'

Superintendent Law would seize the credit, realised Hardiman. And it had really been his idea. But when the time came for the commendations and the celebration drinks, the poor sod who'd had all the work would be forgotten.

Law looked up enquiringly as the sergeant entered the room.

'Well?' he asked.

Hardiman smiled down at the seated man.

'Remember you told me to check that financier's passport?'

'Of course.'

'Nothing wrong with it . . . at first glance.'

'Then what?'

'So I looked further. Checked out the birth certificate, with government records . . .'

Law began to smile, in anticipation.

'According to them, no such person exists,' concluded the sergeant. 'So I put the certificate through to forensic. It's a forgery.'

'Well done, laddie,' praised the superintendent. 'Well done.'

He stood up, taking Charlie's file from those stacked against the wall.

'Routine,' he said softly. 'That's what does it, every time.'

It had taken long enough, thought Hardiman.

'Still not back at the house yet?' Law enquired, expectantly.

'Not yet.'

Law frowned at a sudden thought.

'What about that report from uniformed, their belief there was some sort of observation?'

'Checked on my way here,' said Hardiman. 'Not there any more.'

'Which leaves us with the London firm of underwriters,' said Law. 'I think it's time we checked to see how deeply they investigate their people.'

Onslow Smith looked down contentedly at the file lying before him. Through everything now there was a curt red ink mark: every entry erased. He deserved the comfort of the separate military aircraft that he had arranged for himself, he decided. And it would have been quite wrong anyway to have travelled back with the rest of the team.

He put the documents into the briefcase with the combination lock and placed it alongside the other sealed file holders that would all be taken by courier to the airport for transportation back to America and then oblivion in the C.I.A. archives. In a separate container was the money Wilberforce had insisted on returning. The money would probably upset their computer, he thought; it had already been written off. Just like Wilberforce. Poor bugger.

The telephone surprised him and he stared at it, hesitating before lifting the receiver. He smiled, immediately recognising Braley's voice.

'All aboard?' enquired Smith, cheerily.

'Not quite,' said the man and for the first time Smith realised the apprehension from the other end.

'What do you mean, not quite?'

'I'm sorry I've left it so late,' said Braley. 'I wanted to be sure, so I carried out a complete check . . .'

'For Christ's sake, what is it?' demanded Smith.

'Ruttgers isn't here.'

TWENTY-SEVEN

Edith opened the door without interest, looking dully out into the corridor. Then she saw Charlie and started back. She couldn't make the words and so she just stood there, shaking her head in disbelief.

'Hello,' he said.

'Oh, Charlie . . . Charlie,' she said and all the feelings of the previous days overflowed and she burst into tears.

He came into the room, holding his arms out to her and she clung to him so desperately that he could feel her fingers bruising into his back. He held her as tightly, stroking her hair and her shoulders, trying to calm her, but she couldn't stop, huge sobs racking through her.

Her face muffled into his shoulder, she just kept repeating 'Charlie, oh, Charlie' and he felt her groping at him, needing the physical reassurance of his body.

'It's all right, Edith,' he said, soothingly. 'It's over. All over.'

She wept on and Charlie let her cry, knowing she had to wash the fear and anxiety out of herself. She'd suffered far more than he had, he realised. But he'd make her forget, eventually. Certainly she'd never suffer again, he determined. Never.

Gently he moved her sideways, so they could both sit on the edge of the bed. The crying was becoming less hysterical, he recognised.

'Over, Edith,' he repeated. 'All over.'

It still seemed a long time before she had recovered sufficiently to pull away from him. Her eyes were red and sore and her nose had run. Lovingly, he dried her face. The breath was still jumping unevenly through her, so that her shoulders kept shaking.

'Please kiss me,' she said.

Gently he leaned forward, putting his lips to hers, but when she tried to pull close to him, dragging his mouth towards her in a sudden frenzy, her breath caught again and she had to jerk away, gasping a mixture of laughter and fresh tears.

He put his hands out, holding her face, so she wouldn't collapse.

'Stop it,' he said curtly. 'Stop it, Edith.'

She bit against the emotion, lips tightly closed.

'I'm all right now,' she said, after a while. Still he held her, bringing her forward and lightly kissing her forehead.

'I love you, Edith,' he said.

She smiled up at him, remembering the promise.

'I was so frightened, Charlie,' she said. 'I thought I'd lost you.'

He shook his head.

'They made too many mistakes,' he said.

'You were lucky.'

'Yes,' he agreed seriously. 'They reacted exactly as I thought they would.'

'Let's hide somewhere, Charlie. Somewhere they will never find us.'

'We'll hide,' he said. 'They'll never get this close again.'

'Charlie.'

'What?'

'Make love to me, Charlie. It's been so long.'

Her breath didn't catch and they kissed open-mouthed, trying at the same time to pull the clothes away from each other in urgent tugging movements. They couldn't do it, so they parted briefly, clawing the covering away and then snatched, one for the other, falling back on to the dishevelled bed. The fear that Charlie had kept so tightly controlled surged through him, so that he shuddered as deeply as Edith had done when she'd first seen him and he clung desperately to her, needing the comfort of her body that she'd felt for his earlier. But not sexually, he realised, in sudden, horrified awareness. He crouched over her, flaccid and unresponsive, head buried into her shoulder.

'I *want* to, Edith. I really want to.'

'It doesn't matter.'

'Help me to do it.'

'It won't work, Charlie. Not now.'

'Please.'

'Later, Charlie. It will be better later.'

He toppled sideways, head still into her shoulder so that he couldn't look at her.

'Oh, God, I'm sorry,' he said.

She lay, gently stroking his back. Conscious of how cold he was, she tugged the blanket over them. Because of the confused way they were lying, their legs protruded from the bottom.

'I'm glad,' she said.

He pulled slightly away, still not looking at her.

'Glad?' he said.

'Glad to know you were as scared as me.'

He burrowed into the blanket.

'I was scared,' he admitted, quietly. 'Very scared.'

'And now it's over. For both of us,' she reminded him.

He laughed, an uncertain sound.

'What?' she asked.

'It was supposed to be me, comforting you,' he said.

She pulled his head closer to her, so that his lips were near her breast.

'We need each other very much, don't we, Charlie?' she said, happily.

'Yes,' he said.

'I'm glad you love me, Charlie.'

'Even though I can't prove it?'

'Don't be silly.'

It was growing warm beneath the blanket.

'Your trousers are puddled on the floor,' she said. 'They're going to be very creased.'

'They usually are,' he said, sleepily.

'Yes,' she remembered, 'they usually are. Don't ever alter, will you, Charlie?'

He grunted and she felt his breath deepening against her.

'I love you so much,' she said softly, knowing he couldn't hear her. 'I love you so much.'

She trailed a finger over his cheek, smiling as he twitched at the irritation. It was so good to have him back, she thought. Completely.

It was an hour before he awakened and because he was clinging to her she felt the momentary tightening of his body, until the awareness of where he was registered.

'Hello again,' he said, relaxing.

'Hello.'

'Forgiven me?'

'I told you not to be silly.'

He pulled himself close to the warmth of her body.

'It's good to be with you,' he said.

'Don't ever go away again?'

'Never,' he said.

'Can we leave, straight away?'

He shook his head.

'Get dressed and while we have a celebration meal I'll tell you what else has to be done.'

'Shall we eat here?'

'Too early,' he decided. 'Let's drive somewhere and then take pot luck.'

'All right,' she agreed immediately. He was like a school-boy on the first day of a summer vacation with a five-pound note in his pocket, she thought, rising from the bed and spreading the blanket more fully over him. She knew he was watching her through the bathroom door and turned, smiling.

'You're beautiful, Edith,' he said.

She grew serious, coming to the linking door.

'It is going to be all right, from now on, isn't it, Charlie? No more mistakes . . . no more running?'

'No more mistakes,' he guaranteed.

'I don't think I could go through it again,' she said gravely.

'I promise.'

As if suddenly reminded, Edith stopped, towel in hand, by a travelling bag. It was a large, soft leather case with a shoulder strap and sufficient space to carry anything a person might need on a long journey.

'You'd better have these,' she said, passing over the passports she had drawn from the Zürich bank.

She looked at him expectantly, but Charlie just leaned across the bed, putting them into his jacket pocket. Any conversation about new identities would only rekindle her fear, he decided.

'Hurry,' he urged her. 'It's going to be a great evening.'

Because the car was pointing in that direction, Charlie drove westwards.

'You know,' said Edith, 'for the first time in weeks I feel safe.'

She reached across the tiny car, squeezing his hand.

'So do I,' said Charlie.

It was an hour after they had left that Braley and the American team despatched by Onslow Smith arrived at the hotel, seeking Ruttgers. The man was still registered, agreed the receptionist. But he'd left the hotel. About an hour before. Why didn't they wait?

Superintendent Law and the sergeant had risen to go, pausing in the hallway of Willoughby's apartment.

'It was good of you to see us at home, sir,' said the superintendent.

'You said it was urgent,' Willoughby reminded them.

'And you've no idea why there should be this strange business about the passport?'

Willoughby spread his hands at the question that had been asked already. He was beginning to perspire, he knew.

'Absolutely none,' he said. 'We don't actually check on a person's birth certificate when they become associated with us.'

'Perhaps you should, sir,' said Law. 'You couldn't suggest where we might locate him?'

Again the underwriter made the gesture of helplessness. Another repeated question.

'There was an address abroad . . . Switzerland . . .'

'The Zürich police have already checked, on our behalf,' said Hardiman. 'There hasn't been anyone at the apartment for several days.'

'Then sorry, no,' said Willoughby. So far, he knew he'd kept the concern from his voice. But it was becoming increasingly difficult.

'You will tell us, the moment there is any contact, won't you?' said Law.

'Of course,' Willoughby agreed. 'And I'd appreciate any news that you might get. I don't like the thought of my being involved in something that could be questionable.'

'We will,' said Law, finally opening the door. He paused, looking back at the underwriter.

'The *moment* there is any contact,' he reiterated.

'I understand,' said Willoughby.

'Well?' demanded the superintendent, as they settled into the back of the car that had brought them from Brighton.

'I don't know,' said Hardiman, reflectively. 'According to the checks we asked the Fraud Squad to make, the firm is so straight you could draw lines by it.'

Law nodded.

'Exactly the sort of screen you'd try to hide behind if you were a villain,' said Law.

'Exactly,' agreed Hardiman. 'But without the principals being aware of it.'

'So we're not much farther forward,' said the superintendent.

'What are we going to do?'

Law considered the question.

'Request a meeting with the Chief Constable and if he's agreeable, tomorrow call as big a press conference as possible and name our mystery man as someone to help in our inquiries. It will be the only way to bring him out.'

'The only way,' concurred Hardiman, dutifully.

John Packer was always ready to move at short notice; regarded it as part of being a professional. He'd been late learning of the Fabergé recovery, getting the first hint from a newspaper poster about a jewel haul and then confirming it from the car radio.

He'd approached the house cautiously, alert for any signs that the police were waiting for him. Satisfied, he hadn't bothered to turn off the ignition while he collected his share of the Brighton and Mayfair bank robbery money from the concealed floor-mounted safe in the basement and packed a case.

He'd go north, he decided. He wasn't known in Manchester and it was a big enough place in which to get lost. He was surprised that none of the reports had referred to arrests; he'd have to watch the newspapers closely for the next few days, to establish if he were safe, before attempting a quick flight to the Continent. Amsterdam, he decided. Nice people in Amsterdam.

What had happened to the man with the star-shaped scar? he wondered. He *must* have been nicked. Pity. He'd been bloody good. Odd. But still good.

TWENTY-EIGHT

The meal had been unexciting, but neither Charlie nor Edith had noticed. There had been long periods without conversation, when they'd just stared at each other and twice, aware of the waiter's amused attention, Edith had looked away embarrassed, telling Charlie to stop.

There was still wine left in the half-bottle that he had ordered as the meal began and when the waiter enquired about brandy with the coffee, Charlie refused.

Edith smiled, gratefully.

'Seems like everything has turned out all right,' she said.

'Yes,' agreed Charlie, holding the glass in front of him. 'That's over too.'

'You are sure, aren't you, Charlie?' she asked, expanding the question with sudden urgency. 'Nothing çan go wrong now, can it?'

Charlie reached across, squeezing her hand. She was still frightened, he decided, remembering the doubt with which she had given him the passports at the hotel.

'Willoughby's firm was one of the major Lloyd's insurers,' he said. 'So he was able to be present when the collection was returned to the Russians ... to ask questions without the interest appearing strange. He's never known such official embarrassment.'

'But ...?' she started.

'And I personally saw the surveillance lifted from you.'

She gazed at him, coffee suspended before her.

'What?' she said. Her voice was hollowed out with nervousness.

'There was a team of men assigned to you,' he said gently. 'American. I followed them back to the airport ... they'll be gone by now.'

'I never knew.'

'You weren't supposed to.'

Edith shivered.

'Let's get away from here, Charlie.'

'There's still the Brighton robbery,' he said, calmly. 'And Mayfair, too, although I'm not linked with that as far as the police are concerned.'

'What does that mean?'

'That we can't get out, not immediately. I know who did them, apart from Snare. We can leak the man's name to the police through Willoughby's insurance outlets, like we did that of Wilberforce and Snare with the Fabergé collection.'

'It won't be long, will it, Charlie?'

'Just days, that's all,' he said. 'A week at the most.'

'Then what?'

'Anywhere you choose,' he said. He put the wine glass down, feeling for her hand again.

'Let's go home to bed,' he said.

She answered the pressure of his fingers.

'And I won't fail you there, either,' he added. 'Not this time.'

'That's not important,' said the woman. 'Having you safely back with me, that's important.'

His training had been never to leave a vehicle in a car park, where there was a risk of being boxed in and trapped and Charlie had responded automatically, putting the mini on the edge of an annexe area, immediately adjoining the main road.

He had had to wait at the exit of the restaurant, to receive his change and tip the waiter and so Edith was about five yards ahead of him, walking towards the car, when he left the hotel.

She turned for him to catch up and because it was darker than in the main parking area he didn't at first see the terror spreading over her face. Fear drained the strength from her voice, so the warning came out as little more than a gasp, hardly reaching him at first.

'Charlie,' she said. 'Please God, no, Charlie.'

She came towards him, arms thrown out pleadingly and it

was the movement that completely alerted him. She was staring beyond him, eyes bulged, Charlie realised. He turned back towards the hotel as the woman reached him and saw perfectly in the brighter light Garson Ruttgers spread over the bonnet of the car, his whole body supported, arms triangled out in the officially taught shooting position, left hand clamped against the right wrist to minimise the recoil from the gun.

It took seconds but seemed to unfold in an agonisingly slow motion. The need to snatch up Edith and run fixed itself firmly in his mind and stayed there, isolated, and he wondered why he couldn't react and do such a simple thing.

Then Edith collided with him from behind and he reached out to support her, recognising as he did so that Ruttgers was going to shoot.

The lined, sharp face that Charlie remembered so well from the Kalenin affair tightened against the expected noise and the gun moved up slightly and Charlie even identified it as a heavy weapon, a .375 Magnum.

The explosion and the shock of the impact appeared simultaneous and almost immediately there was the roar of a second shot. Charlie tried to breathe, but couldn't because of the biting pain which numbed his lungs from smashing backwards against the bordering stones of the forecourt. Edith was lying on top of him and he didn't see Ruttgers move. He heard the sound of the car engine, though, and tried to get out from beneath the woman's body and it was then he realised that she was quite motionless and stopped pushing at her.

The crushed breath groaned into him and then wailed up into an anguished moan. The action of supporting Edith had pulled her between them at the moment that Ruttgers had fired and she had taken the full impact of both shots and when Charlie felt up he discovered she didn't have a back any more.

He rolled her away, very gently, crouching over her. The horror had gone from her face. Instead, in death, there was a pleading look, the sort of expression she had had asking him not to go to the cemetery, all those weeks ago.

'Not you, Edith,' he sobbed. 'It shouldn't have been you.'

A shoe had fallen half off her foot, he saw. As if it were important, he reached down and replaced it. And then tried to wipe away a smudge of dirt that had somehow got on to her cheek.

A scream came from the hotel, breaking through to him. He cradled her head against him, very quickly, then carefully lowered her to the ground.

'I've got to run, Edith,' he said. 'Now I've got to.'

Largely governed by instinct, he went low to the car, doubled against recognition. He held the door shut, to avoid any noise, and as he started the engine, he saw just one man walking hesitantly towards the woman's body.

He kept the lights off, so the registration would not be visible, accelerating the car out on to the road in a scurry of gravel. It was difficult to be sure because of the darkened windows of the vehicle, but the man's reactions had been too slow to get anything more than a vague description, Charlie decided.

Which way, he wondered, had Edith's killer gone? It hardly mattered. Ruttgers would have been part of the Crawley hotel surveillance. The part, in his carelessness, he had missed. He'd need a weapon, he decided. It was fortunate he had bothered to examine John Packer's house. Why, he wondered, in the first flood of self-pity, hadn't he shown such detailed caution about everything?

Twenty miles away, on the outskirts of the Sussex village of Cuckfield, Garson Ruttgers stared curiously at the Magnum revolver lying beside him on the passenger seat, then blinked out of the car. Condensation from the exhaust billowed whitely around him, making it difficult to see. A layby, he realised. With a telephone. That was it, a telephone; that's why he'd stopped. He looked back to the gun. He'd done it. Now he had to let those bastards in London know. They'd have to admit he was right, decided Ruttgers, getting unsteadily from the vehicle. Succeeded where Onslow Smith and his team had failed. Get the Directorship back, after this, he thought. Be good, hearing everyone admit how wrong they'd been.

Superintendent Law answered the telephone on the third ring, stretching the sleep from his eyes. Beside him his wife tugged at the bedclothes, showing her annoyance. Irritable cow, he thought.

'Knew you'd want to be told immediately,' said the equally tired voice of Hardiman.

'What?'

'Woman's been shot outside of an hotel on the outskirts of Guildford . . . same name as our financier . . .'

'Dead?'

'Dead.'

Law swung out of bed, ignoring the growing protests of his wife.

'I'll be waiting when you get here,' said the detective.

'I won't be able to sleep again now, not without a pill,' complained the woman, but Law had already closed the bathroom door.

'Damn it,' she said, miserably, dragging the covers over her.

TWENTY-NINE

Apart from Ruttgers, oblivious in his private reverie, everyone sat silently awaiting Onslow Smith's lead.

'Damn,' said the Director. 'Damn, damn, damn.'

With the repetition of every word, he punched hard at the desk, needing physical movement to show his rage and there were isolated shifts of embarrassment from the men watching.

Since they'd arrived at the embassy, Smith had done little but vent his temper in irascible, theatrical gestures, his mind blocked by what had happened.

Apparently aware of the impression he was creating, the Director straightened.

'Right,' he said, as if calling a meeting to order.

The shuffling stopped.

'You're *positive* he hasn't been identified?' demanded Onslow Smith.

'Of course I can't be positive,' said Braley, uncomfortable with the question he had already answered.

He'd been so near, thought Smith, in a sudden flush of remorse. So damn near. And then the fucking paranoid had to go and screw everything up. It would be wrong to let Washington know yet.

'You must have some idea,' he said irritably.

'When we got to the layby,' Braley continued, recounting the familiar story, 'Mr Ruttgers was just sitting in the car ...'

'Just sitting?'

'Yes, sir. Staring straight ahead and doing nothing, except smiling. The engine was still running. And the telephone he'd used to call you was hanging off the hook, where he'd let it drop.'

'The engine still running and there hadn't been a police check?' queried the Director.

'Cuckfield is quite a way from the shooting,' said Braley. 'But it only took us about fifteen minutes from the Crawley hotel.'

'Where the hell was he trying to go?' wondered Smith. He spoke to a bespectacled man on his right.

'Probably never know that,' replied the embassy doctor. 'Perhaps back to the hotel ... perhaps nowhere. Just the urge to get away.'

'How long will he be like that?' asked Smith, nodding towards the immobile figure of the former Director.

'Not long, I shouldn't imagine,' said the doctor. 'I don't think it's anything much more than shock. Could be over in a few hours.'

As if conscious of the attention, Ruttgers suddenly stirred

into life, smiling over at Smith and leaning forward to reinforce the words.

'Killed him,' gloated Ruttgers. 'Shot the bastard, like we should have done weeks ago. Saw him fall. Dead. Charlie Muffin is dead. No need to worry any more . . . dead . . .'

'But . . .' began Braley, who had already had an enquiry made to the police. Smith waved him to silence. Christ knows what mental switchback the correction would make, he thought.

'It could be days before we're able to establish definitely whether Mr Ruttgers was seen sufficiently to be identified,' offered Braley. He'd impressed the Director on this job, he knew. And wanted to go on doing so.

'And we don't have days,' said the Director distantly. But they still had luck, he decided. Only just. But enough to matter; enough to avoid a humiliation as embarrassing as Vienna. Providing he handled it properly. Thank God that even mentally confused, the bloody man had wanted to boast, to prove how much better he was than the rest of them. Without that wild, incoherent contact it wouldn't have been possible to have snatched him off the streets and brought him back to the safety and security of Grosvenor Square.

So he still had the advantage, determined the Director.

Now he had to capitalise upon it. Which meant Ruttgers had to be got out, immediately. And then buried as deeply as possible within some psychiatric clinic.

Smith realised he himself would have to remain in England, and attempt to establish some sort of relationship with whoever was going to succeed George Wilberforce to agree an approach which would satisfy the civilian police.

There would be arguments, Smith anticipated. Bad ones. Maybe even a break between the two services as severe as that which followed the Vienna débâcle. But whatever happened, it would be less embarrassing to America than having a former Director of the C.I.A. arraigned in a British court of law on a charge of murder. That's all he had to consider; keeping America out of it.

He looked up at a movement in front of him and saw the doctor leaning forward, to take a smouldering cigarette from Ruttgers' fingers before it burned low enough to blister him. Ruttgers stirred at the approach, looking around for a replacement. Gently the doctor lit one for him.

'I did it,' suddenly declared Ruttgers, with the bright pride of a child announcing a school prize. 'Everyone else fouled it up, but I did it.'

'Yes,' soothed the doctor. 'You did it.'

'He couldn't have managed it,' said Ruttgers, pointing a nicotine-stained finger at Onslow Smith. 'Not him.'

'Can't you shut him up?' demanded the Director, exasperated.

The doctor turned to him, not bothering to disguise the criticism. 'Is it really doing any harm?' he said.

Smith snorted, twisting the question.

'You wouldn't believe it,' he said, bitterly. 'In a million years, you wouldn't believe it.'

He turned back to Braley, positive again.

'We've got blanket diplomatic clearance,' he said. He indicated the former Director. 'And his name was on the list approved by the Foreign Office. So he leaves. Tonight.'

Seeing the doctor move to speak, Smith hurried on: 'There's an aircraft already laid on ... for me. He can go instead.'

'I think he still might need some medical help,' warned the doctor.

'I'll fix it with the ambassador for you to go as well,' said Smith, anxious to move now he had reached a decision. He'd have to speak to the Secretary of State, he knew. Very soon.

'You will go, of course,' he ordered Braley.

The man nodded in immediate agreement. 'Of course,' he said.

'By this time tomorrow I want nothing to associate us in any way with this,' announced the Director.

'Oh, Christ,' said Braley, softly.

'What's the matter?' demanded Smith, the alarm flaring.

'The hotel at Crawley,' remembered Braley. 'The one in which we were waiting for Mr Ruttgers to return when you called us . . .'

'What about it?'

'The woman stayed there . . . and Mr Ruttgers is registered. With his luggage.'

Beneath the desk, where they couldn't see the tension, Smith gripped and ungripped his hands, fighting against the desire to scream at them for their stupidity. They had had no idea two hours before why he was panicking them from the place and couldn't then have anticipated the danger of not collecting the cases, he remembered. And he'd lost control in front of them sufficiently for one evening, he decided.

'Get your asses back there,' he said, his voice unnaturally soft in his anxiety to contain his anger. 'Get down there and explain that Mr Ruttgers has had to leave, in a hurry. Pay his bill and collect his bags and then get out. And hurry. For God's sake hurry.'

The police would unquestionably uncover the link, he accepted. But by then Ruttgers would be over three thousand miles away and he would have begun negotiations.

'Can we get Ruttgers to London airport by ourselves?' queried Smith, to the doctor.

The bespectacled man nodded, pausing at the doorway. The unexpected flight to Washington upset a lot of arrangements, he realised, annoyed.

'You guys lead an ass-hole of a life, don't you?' he said.

'Yes,' agreed Smith dully. The hotel was an awkward complication, he thought.

'Then why the hell do you do it?' persisted the doctor.

The Director concentrated upon him, fully.

'Sometimes,' he said, 'it seems important.'

But this hadn't been, he decided. Apart from a few inflated egos and a questionable argument about teaching the Russians a lesson, this hadn't been important at all. Quite worthless, in fact.

'How often do you get it right?' asked the doctor.

'Not often enough,' admitted Smith honestly. Suddenly

annoyed at the interrogation, he started up and said, curtly:
'Let's get Ruttgers to the airport, shall we?'

Road blocks would have been established within an hour of
the murder, Charlie knew, sealing a wide area. It had meant
he had had to drive in a circuitous route, impatient at the
amount of time it was taking him to do all that was necessary.

Purposely he was crowding the thoughts into his mind,
trying to blot out the memory of Edith's collapsed, pulped
body.

The Wimbledon house had seemed deserted, he decided.
Where, he wondered, was John Packer? Certainly not
arrested; the garden shed would have been empty after a
police search.

The jewellery recovery had been publicised everywhere.
Panicked then. Panicked and run. The word stayed in his
mind, linking the next thought.

Perhaps, in their panic, they would forget Ruttgers'
luggage. No, he assured himself, in immediate contra-
diction. The connection was too important. Braley wouldn't
overlook something as vital as that. And he'd certainly
appeared in a position of authority at the airport, someone
involved in the final planning. No, Braley would think of
the luggage; it was that sort of professionalism that made
him so good.

Charlie lost the fight against recollection and knuckled
his eyes, trying to clear the blur.

'Shouldn't have been you, Edith,' he said. 'I won't fail ...
even if this goes wrong, I won't fail.'

THIRTY

The improvement in Garson Ruttgers' condition began
almost immediately they left the American embassy and
started through the quiet, early dawn streets of London. By

the time they had cleared the city, he was lighting his own cigarettes and as they neared the airport, he turned to the doctor and asked, quite rationally, if they were going back to America.

When he nodded, Ruttgers turned to Onslow Smith.

'You coming?'

The Director shook his head.

'Then I'll let them know how well it all went,' said Ruttgers.

Smith looked sharply at the man but was stopped by the doctor's warning look.

'Sure,' he said, dismissively. 'You tell them.'

It would take seven hours for the aircraft to reach Washington, calculated Smith. Sufficient time for him to sleep away the fatigue that was gripping his body, before attempting to meet with British officials. It wouldn't be easy, now Wilberforce was gone. Perhaps, he thought, it would be better to arrange through the American ambassador an appointment with somebody in the government. Perhaps, he thought, the Secretary of State would insist upon taking control. There'd be a lot of anxiety in Washington when he told them.

He swayed at the sudden movement of the car and realised they had turned off the motorway.

'I hardly think there's any need for me to go,' said the doctor, in hopeful protest.

Smith looked at Ruttgers before replying.

'I think there is,' he insisted. 'It's a long flight.'

The internal injury would be intensive, Smith knew. And he was going to make damned sure that he closed every avenue of criticism that he could, even down to something as minor as having the man accompanied back to Washington by a physician.

'I really don't think there's much wrong with him,' said the doctor.

'You can be back here by tomorrow,' said Smith, closing the conversation. He had more to worry about than the feelings of an embassy doctor, decided Smith. It was his future career he was trying to save.

They looped off before the tunnel, taking the peripheral road to the private section. Soon, thought Onslow Smith. It would all be over very soon.

Because of the twenty-four-hour activity at the airport, there were several cars in the staff park and the darkened mini was quite inconspicuous as the limousine swept by.

Despite the growing daylight, lights still held the building in a yellow glow. The driver had already spoken into the radio and as they pulled in front of the embarkation lounge, marines and airport security men moved out into a pre-arranged position, closing off the area. Others arranged themselves loosely around the aircraft, an inner protection for the people boarding.

'I missed the announcement,' said the doctor, uncaring now in his anger. 'What time did the war start?'

Smith looked at him, shaking his head.

The chauffeur opened the door and Smith got out, leaving the doctor to help Ruttgers.

'Anything more?' enquired the driver.

'Wait for me,' instructed Smith. 'We'll see the plane away.'

The chauffeur re-entered the car, moving it to the designated parking area alongside the buildings and Smith smiled mechanically at the customs and immigration officials who approached.

Smith had arranged the papers in his briefcase during the journey and produced the authorisations as they were requested.

'Seems a lot of activity,' suggested the customs officer.

'Yes,' agreed Smith.

'No need for me to see anything, is there?' asked the man.

'No,' agreed Smith. 'No need at all. Just personal belongings, nothing more.'

They turned at the hurried arrival of the second car. Braley misjudged the last corner, actually scuffing stones and dust against the barrier wall.

Braley took the vehicle almost to where his superior was talking to the officials.

'The baggage,' Smith identified it, as Braley got out of the car.

'Fine,' said the customs man.

'No need for me to delay you either,' said the immigration official. 'Thank you.'

'Thank you,' responded Smith, politely.

The men who had gone with Braley were already unloading the luggage, he saw, turning to the car.

He waited until the British officials were sufficiently far away, then demanded urgently: 'Well?'

'Absolutely no trouble,' Braley assured him.

'The police hadn't got there then?'

'No.'

Breath was rasping into the man. He'd made a complete recovery, decided Braley.

The Director turned to where Ruttgers and the doctor were waiting.

'Let's get him away,' he said. It was still going to be all right, he thought, in a sudden burst of euphoria.

Ruttgers followed a military steward up the steps, taking without question the wide, double seat that the man indicated to the left side of the aisle. The doctor belted himself into the seat immediately to the right and then looked up at Onslow Smith.

'Call me at the embassy, from Washington,' ordered the Director.

'There'll be nothing to report,' said the doctor, truculently. Behaving like a lot of kids, he thought, irritably.

'Call me anyway. I want to know he got there safely.'

'O.K.'

Smith turned back to where Braley and his men were coming aboard, stacking the luggage they had collected from the Crawley hotel into seats at the rear and then spreading themselves around the aircraft.

'Thank you,' said Smith to Braley. 'You did very well.'

The man smiled at the praise. His breathing was easier.

'Want me to stay with him all the way?' he enquired, nodding towards Ruttgers.

'All the way,' confirmed the Director. 'You're being routed through to the Andrews Air Base. There'll be an ambulance waiting when you arrive, to take over from the doctor.'

The man nodded.

'And Braley?'

'Yes, sir.'

'I've been impressed with the way you work. Very impressed. I think we can establish a working relationship when all this is over.'

'Thank you,' said Braley.

There was movement from the front of the aircraft and Smith looked up to see the co-pilot nodding.

'I'll see you in a few days,' said Smith, automatically.

'Good luck,' responded Braley.

'I'll need it,' said Smith, caught by the expression.

Men were standing by the ramp as he descended, to wheel it away. He hurried to the doorway of the building, where the chauffeur was waiting with a coat. Smith pulled it on and they both turned to watch the aircraft start its take-off manoeuvre, taxiing out on to the slip runway.

Inside the plane, the steward ensured that Ruttgers had his seat-belt secured and then sat down for take-off in the seat immediately in front.

'I'm hungry,' Ruttgers announced.

The steward turned, smiling politely at the man he'd been told was a government official of high rank who was suffering a mental collapse.

'There's food on board,' he said. 'I'll be serving it once we've taken off.'

At the rear, Braley's team were already sprawled out, eyes closed. Only Braley remained awake, staring up the aircraft at Ruttgers. It was a pity, the man decided. A damned pity. Ruttgers had his faults, but he'd once been a very good Director. He didn't deserve a back-door hustle to some sanatorium, just because a few people in Washington needed protection. Braley closed his eyes, reflectively. So Charlie had escaped for the second time. But not as cleanly as in Vienna. How badly would he be affected by his wife's death? he wondered. Probably, thought Braley, he was one of the few people caught up in the Vienna operation who didn't hate Charlie Muffin. Perhaps because he had known him so well. He smiled at the sudden thought. Actually, he decided, he was quite glad Charlie had slipped away again.

The plane began its take-off run and then snatched up. Braley opened his eyes and looked out at the fast-disappearing ground. The sodium lights still stretched away from the airport like yellow strands of a spider's web. It looked very peaceful and calm, he thought.

As the aircraft's climb flattened out, the steward unclipped his belt and stood up, smiling down again at Ruttgers.

'I'll get you something to eat,' he said.

The man was staring up at the light forbidding smoking and the moment it was extinguished began groping into his pocket. Gratefully, he flipped open the top and then turned, frowning at the doctor, holding out the empty packet like a spoiled child showing an exhausted sweet bag.

'Don't smoke,' apologised the doctor.

'In my grip,' said Ruttgers. 'There's a carton in my grip.'

The steward was even farther back, in the galley, the doctor realised. He unfastened his belt and walked down to Ruttgers' luggage. An armrest had been removed and the seat-belts from two places adjusted through the straps for take-off safety. The doctor disentangled them, then stood frowning. Finally he picked up two shoulder bags and walked back up the aisle, holding them stretched out before him.

'We're still climbing. Do you mind sitting down,' the steward called out, from behind.

The doctor smiled, apologetically, then looked back to Ruttgers.

'Which one?' he asked Ruttgers.

The former Director hesitated, frowning his confusion and the doctor immediately wondered at a relapse. Curiously Ruttgers reached out for the soft black leather bag that Edith had used during her trip from Zürich and over which Charlie, hands shaking with emotion and urgency, had worked upon five hours before in the Crawley hotel, after returning from the Wimbledon home of John Packer.

'Don't understand,' mumbled Ruttgers.

The doctor realised the difficulty the man was having assembling his thoughts and turned towards his own bag, on the adjoining seat. There was some Vallium, he knew. That's all the man needed, he was sure. Just a tranquilliser.

Ruttgers scraped back the zip and looked inside. Lodged on top of the dirty clothing was a hard, black rectangle. Ruttgers turned it, then opened the passport that Charlie had used for the two years since the Vienna disaster.

'Him!' shouted Ruttgers, loud enough to awaken the sleeping men behind, thrusting the passport towards the startled doctor and trying to snatch the clothes out of the bag.

At that moment, the pilot levelled further, at one thousand feet sufficiently away from the noise restrictions of the airport, and the first of the pressure devices that Charlie had taken from Packer's home and triggered for that height detonated the plastic explosive.

The jet jumped and momentarily appeared to those watching on the ground to hang suspended. Then it sagged, where the explosion had shattered the fuselage in half and as the two sections fell away the full cargo of fuel erupted in a huge ball of yellow and blue flame.

Charlie was already out of the car park, needing the initial confusion to avoid detection from the people statued four hundred yards away, gazing open-mouthed into the sky.

The movement of the small car was quite undetected.

As he headed eastwards along the M-4 towards London,

fire engines from Hounslow and Feltham blared in the opposite direction, sirens at full volume, blue lights flashing.

It was too much to think that Ruttgers might have looked into the bag, decided Charlie.

THIRTY-ONE

Superintendent Law had telephoned from London, so when he swept white-faced into the office, Hardiman had all the files from the Brighton robbery carefully parcelled and waiting on the tables against the wall.

The sergeant stood uncertainly, frowning at the men who followed the superintendent into the room.

'There they are,' said Law, sweeping his hand towards them.

'What . . . ?' questioned Hardiman, but Law waved the hand again, stopping him.

The strangers began carrying the files from the office. They didn't speak to each other and Superintendent Law didn't speak to them. It took a very short time.

'You'll want a receipt?' said one of the men.

'Yes,' said Law.

Quickly the man scribbled on to a pad and handed it over.

'Thank you for your co-operation,' he said.

Law didn't reply.

'What the hell has happened?' demanded the sergeant, as the room emptied.

Law slammed the door, turning to stand immediately in front of it.

'That,' he said, a vein throbbing at his temple in his anger, 'was the beginning of the big cover-up.'

'I don't understand,' said Hardiman.

'Neither do I, not completely,' admitted the superintendent. 'Nor am I being allowed to.'

'But what *happened*?' repeated Hardiman.

Law walked away from the door, seating himself with elaborate care behind the desk and then staring down at it, assembling the words.

'In Whitehall,' he started. 'There were separate meetings. First the Chief Constables of Surrey, Sussex and Kent were taken into an office and addressed by God knows who. Then we were taken into another room and told that the whole thing had been taken over by a government department and that as far as we were concerned, the cases were closed.'

The vein increased its vibrations.

'Cases?'

'The Brighton robbery. And the shooting.'

'But you can't just close a million pounds robbery. And a murder,' protested Hardiman. 'That's ridiculous.'

'Yes,' agreed Law. 'It is, isn't it? But you can, apparently, if it's felt sufficiently important for national security. And that's the bullshit we've been fed, all day ... a question of national security and official secrets.'

'But what about ... what about the money?' floundered the sergeant, with too many questions to ask.

'Everyone who suffered a loss will be compensated by the Clearing Houses ... who I suppose will receive their instructions like we received ours today.'

'But how shall we mark the files?'

Law snorted, waving towards the door.

'What files?'

'I don't believe it,' said Hardiman, slumping down.

'No,' said Law. 'Neither do I. Incidentally, because of your close involvement, you're to see the Chief Constable at four this afternoon.'

'What for?'

'To be told, presumably, that if you disclose anything of what happened to anyone, you'll be transgressing the Official Secrets Act.'

'But what about that damned man's passport ... the one that was found with all that other stuff after the crash? It was a direct link. It was all tidied up: the robbery, the murder, the air crash . . .'

Law shook his head. 'We are told that no explanation could be made, other than that it was part of an attempt . . . an attempt which failed . . . to discredit Britain. I don't think that a complete account was even given to the Chief Constables.'

Hardiman laughed, suspiciously.

'Attempt to discredit Britain by whom?'

Law made an irritable movement.

'Ask the Chief Constable this afternoon, perhaps he knows.'

'Does it mean the bloody man is dead?'

'I presume so,' said Law. 'Perhaps he was being taken to America in the aircraft. I don't really know. We weren't allowed to ask questions.'

The superintendent's annoyance thrust him from the chair and he began walking around the office without direction.

'What are you going to do?' asked Hardiman.

Law smiled at him, a crooked expression.

'Resign, you mean?' he queried. He shook his head. 'In another two years I'll have got my thirty in. Do you think I'm going to chuck up a pension, just for this?'

'No,' accepted Hardiman. 'I suppose not.'

'But I'd like to,' added the superintendent, softly. 'Christ, I'd like to. Can you imagine how frightened they'd be by that?'

He looked up at the sergeant, throwing his arms out helplessly.

'The way they use people!' he protested. 'What gives them the right to use people like . . . like they didn't matter?'

'Power,' said Hardiman, cynically. 'Just power.'

'Wouldn't it be nice,' reflected the detective, 'to know that just occasionally it all gets cocked up?'

'For them it never does,' said Hardiman. 'Not enough,

anyway. There's usually too many people between them and personal disaster.'

'Yes,' said Law. 'People like us.'

'So,' said Hardiman, positively. 'What do we do now?'

'The official orders,' recited the superintendent, 'are to conclude the matter, bringing to an immediate close any outstanding parts of the investigation.'

The sergeant glanced over at the empty file tables.

'Are there any outstanding parts?'

'The underwriter, Willoughby, is probably wondering where his mysterious investor is ... he's obviously been used, like everybody else ...'

He moved towards his coat.

'And the journey will do me good. I don't want to stay around a police station any more today. I might be reminded about justice and stupid things like that.'

'What are you going to tell Willoughby?'

Law turned at the door.

'The way I feel at the moment,' he said, 'I feel like telling him everything I know.'

'But you won't,' anticipated the sergeant.

'No,' agreed Law. 'I won't. I'll do what I'm told and wait another two years to collect a pension. Don't forget that four o'clock appointment.'

The tiredness dragged at Smallwood's face and occasionally the hand that lay along the arm of the chair gave a tiny, convulsive twitch.

'Well?' demanded the Foreign Secretary.

The Premier made a dismissive movement.

'There's an enormous amount of police annoyance,' he said. 'But that was to be expected.'

'Will they obey the instructions?'

'They'll have to,' said Smallwood. 'The Official Secrets Act is a useful document. Thank God none of them knows the complete story.'

'What about America?'

Smallwood shifted in his chair.

'They made the bigger mistakes this time. We agreed to cover for them.'

'So hopefully not too much damage has been caused?' said Heyden.

'Not too much,' agreed Smallwood.

THIRTY-TWO

The grief would always be there, Willoughby knew. In time, he supposed, Charlie would learn to build a shell around it, a screen behind which he would be able completely to hide. It wouldn't happen yet though. Not for months; maybe more. The amount of time, perhaps, that it would take his own feelings to subside.

'I was wrong,' announced the underwriter. It seemed so long, he thought, since had had practised the honesty upon which Charlie had once commented.

Charlie looked up, the concentration obviously difficult.

'In thinking I would do anything to help you,' expanded Willoughby. 'Even though we talked about it, on that first day here in this office. I still didn't believe it would result in that sort of slaughter.'

When Charlie said nothing, the underwriter demanded; 'Do you realise there were twelve people on that plane ... a total of twelve people killed?'

'Thirteen,' reminded Charlie. 'Don't forget Edith died.'

'An eye for an eye, a tooth for a tooth,' quoted Willoughby. 'I can't accept that biblical equation, Charlie. Can you?'

'Yes,' said Charlie, simply. 'I can. I don't expect you to. But I can.'

'With no regrets at all?'

William Braley had been on the plane, remembered Charlie.

'I would have preferred to kill just one man ... the man responsible,' he said. 'But that wasn't possible.'

He straightened, sloughing off the apathy.

'Your father disliked killing, too,' he went on, staring directly at Willoughby. 'And avoided it, whenever it was possible, just as he taught me to avoid it. But sometimes it isn't possible. We didn't make the rules . . .'

'Rules!' exclaimed Willoughby, infusing the word with disgust and refusing Charlie's defence. 'Is that what it was, Charlie? Some sort of obscene game? Do you imagine Edith would have wanted that sort of revenge?'

Charlie looked evenly across the desk at the outraged man. It was proper that Willoughby should feel like this, he decided. There was no point in trying to convince him. At least he fully understood it now.

'No,' he replied softly, abandoning the explanation. 'Edith wouldn't have wanted it. But I did.'

Willoughby shook his head, exasperated.

'The police found your passport, you know. Just slightly charred. Superintendent Law told me. They've closed the case, incidentally. I inferred the civil police believe you were on board . . . you're probably freer now than you've been since Vienna.'

'Oh,' said Charlie, uninterested.

'Why *did* you do that?' asked Willoughby. 'If they'd found your passport, in a bag that shouldn't have been aboard, then Ruttgers would have lived.'

'No,' said Charlie, definitely. 'That's why the passport and Edith's bag *were* important.'

Willoughby sat, waiting. It would only increase the man's disgust, realised Charlie. It didn't seem to matter.

Sighing, he went on: 'The bomb that destroyed the aircraft wasn't in Edith's bag. There were two other bombs, both in separate pieces of Ruttger's own luggage. I wasn't able to get near enough to the aircraft to see what sort of baggage checks were being conducted. So I had to create a dummy . . . something that could have been discarded, if there had been any sort of examination. In fact, there wasn't.'

'That's horrifying,' said Willoughby. He seemed to have

187

difficulty in continuing, then said at last: 'Did my father teach you to think like that, as well?'

'Yes,' confirmed Charlie simply.

'And I thought I knew him,' said Willoughby sadly.

'I'm sorry that you became so deeply involved,' Charlie apologised. 'It was wrong of me to endanger you as much as I did.'

'I would have refused, had I known it was going to turn out like this,' said the underwriter.

'Of course you would,' said Charlie.

'What are you going to do now?'

'It's over a month since the headstone went up on Edith's grave,' he said. 'Those laburnum trees are very near and they stain . . .'

'I didn't mean that,' corrected Willoughby.

'I know,' said Charlie. 'But that's as far ahead as I want to think, at the moment.'

He rose, moving towards the door.

'I saw a man working on a grave when we met that day near your father's tomb. He'd maintained it in a beautiful condition. I want to keep Edith's just like that.'

'Charlie,' said Willoughby.

He turned.

'Keep in touch?' asked the underwriter.

'Maybe.'

'I was wrong to criticise,' admitted Willoughby. 'I know they weren't your rules . . .'

Charlie ignored the attempted reconciliation. It might come later, he supposed.

'They won, you know,' he said. 'Wilberforce and Ruttgers and God knows who else were involved. They really won.'

'Yes, Charlie,' said Willoughby. 'I know they did.'

'We were damned lucky, Willard.'

'Yes, Mr President. Damned lucky.'

Henry Austin pushed the chair back and stretched his feet out on to the Oval Office desk.

'Can you imagine what the Russians would have done if they'd found the stuff that fell out of the plane?'

'It's too frightening to think about.'

'Thank Christ the British were so helpful.'

'I think they were as embarrassed as we were.'

The telephone of the appointments secretary lit up on the President's console.

'The new C.I.A. Director is here, Mr President,' said the secretary.

'Send him in,' ordered Austin.

THIRTY-THREE

Although the last snows of winter had thawed and it was officially spring, few other people had opened their dachas yet, preferring still the central heating of Moscow. Berenkov had lit a fire and stood, with the warmth on his back, in his favourite position overlooking the capital.

He heard the sound of glasses and turned as Valentina came towards him.

'It was kind of Comrade Kalenin to give you this French wine,' said the woman.

'He knows how much I like it,' said Berenkov. He sipped, appreciatively.

'Excellent,' he judged.

His wife smiled at his enjoyment, joining him at the window.

'So she died, as well?' said Valentina, suddenly.

Berenkov nodded. The woman's interest in the Charlie Muffin affair had equalled his, he realised.

'We've positive confirmation that it was her,' he said.

'But not about him?'

'Enough,' said Berenkov. 'There's really little doubt.'

Neither spoke for several moments and then Valentina said: 'That's good.'

189

'Good?'

'Now there won't be the sort of suffering that you and I would understand,' explained the woman.

'No,' agreed Berenkov. 'There won't be any suffering.'

One thousand five hundred miles away, in a cemetery on the outskirts of Guildford, Charlie Muffin scrubbed methodically back and forth, pausing occasionally to pick the red and yellow laburnum pods from among the green stone chips.

A Selection of Arrow Bestsellers

Bestselling Thriller/Suspense

☐ Voices on the Wind	Evelyn Anthony	£2.50
☐ See You Later, Alligator	William F. Buckley	£2.50
☐ Hell is Always Today	Jack Higgins	£1.75
☐ Brought in Dead	Harry Patterson	£1.95
☐ The Graveyard Shift	Harry Patterson	£1.95
☐ Maxwell's Train	Christopher Hyde	£2.50
☐ Russian Spring	Dennis Jones	£2.50
☐ Nightbloom	Herbert Lieberman	£2.50
☐ Basikasingo	John Matthews	£2.95
☐ The Secret Lovers	Charles McCarry	£2.50
☐ Fletch	Gregory Mcdonald	£1.95
☐ Green Monday	Michael M. Thomas	£2.95
☐ Someone Else's Money	Michael M. Thomas	£2.50
☐ Albatross	Evelyn Anthony	£2.50
☐ The Avenue of the Dead	Evelyn Anthony	£2.50

ARROW BOOKS, BOOKSERVICE BY POST, PO BOX 29, DOUGLAS, ISLE OF MAN, BRITISH ISLES

NAME ....

ADDRESS ....

....

....

Please enclose a cheque or postal order made out to Arrow Books Ltd. for the amount due and allow the following for postage and packing.

U.K. CUSTOMERS: Please allow 22p per book to a maximum of £3.00.

B.F.P.O. & EIRE: Please allow 22p per book to a maximum of £3.00.

OVERSEAS CUSTOMERS: Please allow 22p per book.

Whilst every effort is made to keep prices low it is sometimes necessary to increase cover prices at short notice. Arrow Books reserve the right to show new retail prices on covers which may differ from those previously advertised in the text or elsewhere.